Here's what kids and grown-ups have to say about the Magic Tree House® books:

"Oh, man . . . the Magic Tree House series is really exciting!"
—Christina

"I like the Magic Tree House series. I stay up all night reading them. Even on school nights!"
—Peter

"Jack and Annie have opened a door to a world of literacy that I know will continue throughout the lives of my students."
—Deborah H.

"As a librarian, I have seen many happy young readers coming into the library to check out the next Magic Tree House book in the series."
—Lynne H.

MAGIC TREE HOUSE®
SUPER EDITION
#1 WORLD AT WAR, 1944

Previously published as *Danger in the Darkest Hour*

BY MARY POPE OSBORNE

ILLUSTRATED BY SAL MURDOCCA

A STEPPING STONE BOOK™

Random House New York

In memory of my father, Colonel William P. Pope, who fought in World War II

Visit us on the Web!
MagicTreeHouse.com
SteppingStonesBooks.com

Educators and librarians, for a variety of teaching tools, visit us at RHTeachersLibrarians.com

The Library of Congress has cataloged the hardcover edition of this work as follows:
Osborne, Mary Pope.
Danger in the darkest hour / Mary Pope Osborne. — Magic tree house super edition.
pages cm.
Summary: "The magic tree house has taken Jack and Annie back in time to England in 1944. England is fighting for its life in World War II. Before long, Jack and Annie find themselves parachuting into Normandy, France, behind enemy lines. The date is June 5. Will the brave brother and sister team be able to make a difference during one of the darkest times in history?" —Provided by publisher.
ISBN 978-0-553-50885-7 (trade) — ISBN 978-0-553-49773-1 (lib. bdg.) — ISBN 978-1-5247-6652-8 (ebook)
1. World War, 1939–1945—Campaigns—France—Normandy—Juvenile fiction. [1. World War, 1939–1945—Campaigns—France—Normandy—Fiction. 2. Time travel—Fiction. 3. Magic—Fiction. 4. Brothers and sisters—Fiction.] I. Title.
PZ7.O81167Dan 2015 [Fic]—dc23 2014021739

ISBN 978-0-553-50885-7 (pbk.)

Printed in the United States of America
10

This book has been officially leveled by using the F&P Text Level Gradient™ Leveling System.

CONTENTS

Prologue

One summer day in Frog Creek, Pennsylvania, a mysterious tree house appeared in the woods. It was filled with books. A boy named Jack and his sister, Annie, found the tree house and soon discovered that it was magic. They could go to any time and place in history just by pointing to a picture in one of the books. While they were gone, no time at all passed back in Frog Creek.

Jack and Annie eventually found out that the tree house belonged to Morgan le Fay, a magical librarian from the legendary realm of Camelot. They have since traveled on many adventures in the magic tree house and completed many missions for both Morgan le Fay and her friend Merlin the magician. Teddy and Kathleen, two young enchanters from Camelot, have sometimes helped Jack and Annie in both big and small ways.

Now Jack and Annie are about to receive an unexpected call for help. . . .

ONE

COMMANDO

"Jack!" Annie shouted from the front yard.

Jack looked up from his book. Tired from a soccer game, he was lying on his bed, reading about volcanoes on Mars. Late-afternoon shadows stretched across his room.

"Jack! *JACK!*"

Jack stood up and crossed to the window. Annie was standing by her bike. A towel was draped around her neck; her hair was wet from swimming in the lake. She was looking up at the sky as if she was searching for something.

"What do you want?" Jack called through the screen.

"Come down!" she called. "Help me look."

"Look for what?" said Jack.

"Just come! You won't believe it!" said Annie.

Jack sighed. He marked his place in his book and went downstairs to the front porch. "This better be good," he said. "I was in the middle of a book."

Annie was still looking up at the sky. "Where did he go?" she said.

"Where did *who* go?" said Jack.

Annie didn't answer. She walked to the edge of the yard and kept looking. "Oh, darn, I don't see him!"

"See who?" said Jack. "What are you talking about?"

"The pigeon!" said Annie.

Jack stared at Annie for a moment. "Seriously?" he said. "You're looking for a *pigeon*?"

"Yes!"

"You called me away from my book to see a *pigeon*?" said Jack.

"Yes! Help me find him!" Annie said.

Jack rolled his eyes and stepped into the yard. He looked up at the hazy sky.

"He was following me. He swooped down near my head," said Annie, still looking in every direction. "I don't see him now. Where could he have gone?"

"What's the big deal?" said Jack. "We see pigeons every day."

"Not like this one," said Annie. "When I was getting on my bike at the lake, I heard a loud cooing. I looked up—he was sitting on a branch, and he looked straight into my eyes. He was super-intelligent, I could tell."

"Are you sure you weren't out in the sun too long?" asked Jack.

"I'm serious," said Annie. "He had these intense staring eyes. I talked to him, like I said 'hi,' and then he took off. I thought, *okay, so much for that*. But then I started riding home and he flew in front of me—right across my path!"

"How do you know it was the same pigeon?" asked Jack.

"I just know. He circled above me all the way home!" said Annie. "He even swooped down a couple more times. But I don't see him now. . . . I don't see him at all. . . ." Her voice trailed off as she looked up at the sky and around the yard.

"Well, that's enough pigeon-hunting for me," said Jack. "I'm heading back to my book." He turned to go inside.

"Ahh! I see him! I see him!" Annie whispered.

Jack stopped. "Where?"

"There!" Annie pointed to a plump pigeon perched on a bird feeder that was hanging from a maple tree. She stepped toward him. The pigeon didn't move. She stepped closer and closer. The bird still didn't move. "Oh, wow, Jack. You won't believe this—I didn't see it until now."

"What? See what?" said Jack.

"Oh, wow, oh, wow," Annie whispered.

Jack walked slowly toward Annie. When he reached her side, he stopped and stared at the bird, too. It was an ordinary-looking pigeon: smoky gray with black stripes on his wings and iridescent-green neck feathers. His amber-colored eyes stared at Jack.

"Look at his leg," Annie whispered.

Attached to one of the pigeon's spindly legs was a tiny red canister. "Whoa," whispered Jack. "I think he's a carrier pigeon."

"A carrier pigeon?" said Annie.

"Yeah, they carried messages to people a long time ago," said Jack. "There used to be lots of them, but not anymore."

"Why not?" Annie asked.

"They're not needed anymore," said Jack. "Not with technology like the Internet and cell phones."

The pigeon made a low cooing sound.

"Why did he follow you?" said Jack. "And where'd he come from?"

Annie took a deep breath. "I know where he came from. I just figured it out," she said.

"Where?"

"Another time," said Annie. "A time before the Internet and cell phones."

Jack's heart skipped a beat. "You think?"

"I *know*," said Annie. "And the message is for us!" She moved a step closer toward the pigeon. But the bird flapped his wings and took off from the feeder. Then he soared out of their yard and up the street, disappearing into the trees of the Frog Creek woods.

"Let's go!" cried Annie.

"Wait, I'll get my pack." Jack bolted into the house, grabbed his backpack from the hallway, and hurried outside.

Jack and Annie raced up the sidewalk. They crossed the street and ran into the woods. As they weaved in and out of dark-green shadows, the late-summer air smelled of sun-dried wood and fallen pine needles. Birds called lazily from the treetops.

Finally they stopped at the base of the tallest oak.

"Of course," said Annie.

She grabbed the rope ladder that dangled from the treetop and started up. Jack followed and they both scrambled inside the magic tree house. Golden sunlight lit the stacks of books and the shimmering *M* in the floor.

"Of course," said Jack.

A soft cooing sound came from the window. The carrier pigeon was pacing on the windowsill.

"Of course a million times," said Annie, laughing. "Don't fly away. I won't hurt you, I promise."

The pigeon stopped pacing and stared at her with his amber eyes.

"I can take that message from you now," Annie whispered, "if you don't mind."

"He doesn't mind," said Jack. "He's a professional."

"Right," said Annie. The pigeon was very still as Annie reached out and gently opened the lid of the red canister attached to his leg. She pulled out a tiny scroll. Then she snapped the lid shut and unrolled the piece of paper.

Annie and Jack looked at the writing together. It wasn't elegant like Merlin's or Morgan le Fay's writing—it was the scrawl of a kid's handwriting. Jack looked at the signature. "It's from Teddy," he said.

"Uh-oh," said Annie. "What happened? Did he goof up again?"

"I'll bet he did," said Jack. They both laughed. The apprentice sorcerer from Camelot often made them laugh. Sometimes he made big mistakes when he tried to do magic. Many of the mistakes were funny, but a few had been terrible.

Annie read the letter aloud:

Dear Jack and Annie,
I sent Commando to find you.

"Commando?" Jack interrupted. "That's a funny name for a Camelot pigeon."

"Yeah, it sounds like a tough army guy," Annie said. She kept reading:

> Kathleen and I are working with the forces of good in one of the darkest hours of history. And we need your help.
>
> Please come to Glastonbury, England. Right now.
>
> Your friend,
> Teddy

"I can't wait to see Teddy and Kathleen," said Annie.

"Yeah," said Jack. He was especially excited to see Kathleen, a brilliant and beautiful young enchantress from Camelot. "But what does Teddy mean—'one of the darkest hours of history'?"

Annie shrugged.

The pigeon made a low cooing sound.

"Commando wants us to hurry," said Annie.

"Okay. Let's go," Jack said. He took another deep breath and pointed to the words *Glastonbury,*

England on the tiny piece of paper. "I wish we could go there."

The wind started to blow.

The tree house started to spin.

It spun faster and faster.

Then everything was still.

Absolutely still.

TWO

Top-Secret

Commando cooed as if saying good-bye. Then he flapped his wings and flew out of the tree house. He disappeared into the misty gray twilight.

"Thanks, Commando!" Annie called after him.

"Well, I guess we're here," said Jack, shivering in the chilly air. "But our clothes didn't change. I wonder why."

The tree house had landed in the branches of a tall maple tree. Through the haze, Jack and Annie could see ducks floating on a pond and sheep grazing in a meadow bordered by hedgerows. Beyond the hedges were broken-down buildings—stone pillars and crumbling archways. There was no sign of people.

"It looks ancient," said Annie. "Is Glastonbury part of Camelot?"

"I don't know," said Jack.

"This looks sort of like Camelot," said Annie.

"Yeah, the *ruins* of Camelot," said Jack.

"Teddy! Kathleen!" Annie called.

There was no answer.

"Let's go look for them," said Jack.

Jack grabbed his backpack. He and Annie climbed down the rope ladder. They stepped onto the wet grass and started across the meadow. Rounding a hedge, they came upon the remains of what had once been a huge church. The roofless building had tall ivy-covered walls and grand arches made of stone blocks.

"Cheerio, friends!" A teenage boy strode through one of the arches. The boy wore an old-fashioned flight suit, gloves, and a tight-fitting leather helmet. He carried a khaki duffel bag.

"Teddy!" cried Annie. She and Jack hurried to the young enchanter of Camelot. Teddy put down his bag, and they all hugged.

"I am glad Commando found you!" said Teddy. "He is quite a smashing soldier, you know."

"Who? The pigeon?" said Annie.

"Yes. Commando is a member of the National Pigeon Service," said Teddy.

Jack and Annie giggled. "You're kidding, right?" said Jack.

"Not at all," said Teddy. "Pigeon breeders have given over two hundred thousand pigeons to the British military to carry messages throughout Europe. Commando has been on dozens of missions. The missions were all in *this* time, of course. He needed the tree house to take him to *your* time."

"So what *is* this time?" asked Jack.

"It is June fourth, 1944," said Teddy. "And you have landed in Glastonbury, England. It is the site of one of the great monasteries of Europe.

"Teddy put down his bag, and they all hugged."

You can still see an ancient tower on the sacred hill of Glastonbury Tor." He pointed to a conical hill overlooking the flat countryside. "Eventually all the sacred buildings fell into ruin, but legends of King Arthur still surround this area. For that reason, I thought it might be a good place to meet you—a living midpoint between our worlds."

"Where's Kathleen?" asked Annie, looking around. "We thought she would be with you."

"Well, that is why I called for you," said Teddy. "But first, how much do you know about World War Two?"

Jack gasped. "Did we come to the time of World War Two?"

"I am afraid you have. The war has been going on for almost five years," said Teddy.

"Oh, man," said Jack.

"So you know about World War Two?" said Teddy.

"Some," said Jack. "I know that America fought Germany and Italy and Japan. And a man named

Adolf Hitler was the leader of Germany. And his political party was called the Nazis."

"And we also know that three of our great-grandfathers fought in World War Two," said Annie.

"The people of England are grateful for all the help the Americans are giving them fighting this war," said Teddy. "At this point, Nazis have taken over most of Europe. They have killed countless innocent civilians, including millions of Jewish people."

"That's terrible," said Annie.

"Really terrible," said Jack. "But what does this war have to do with you and Kathleen?"

"When Merlin looked into the future, he saw this frightful time," said Teddy. "He saw how important it was to bring hope to British leaders. So he sent Kathleen and me to London."

"The leaders actually met with you?" asked Jack.

Teddy smiled. "Indeed they did," he said.

"Kathleen used a bit of magic to make us both appear older than we are. We were quite brilliant, wearing the right disguises and using the right manners and speech. We seem to have inspired everyone, including the prime minister, Winston Churchill."

"Really?" said Jack.

"Oh, yes," said Teddy. "In fact, Winston inducted Kathleen and me into the SOE."

"What's that?" asked Annie.

"SOE stands for Special Operations Executive," said Teddy. "It is a top-secret organization that Winston formed. It conducts undercover missions in countries occupied by the Nazis. In the short time since Kathleen and I completed the required training, we have both been sent on many secret assignments."

"Is Kathleen away on an assignment now?" asked Annie.

"Yes. Kathleen left for a mission in France more than three weeks ago. And now . . ." Teddy stopped.

"And now what?" asked Jack.

"Now it seems she has disappeared," said Teddy.

"Oh, no! What happened to her?" asked Annie.

"I do not know," said Teddy.

"What was her mission?" asked Jack.

"I do not know that, either. She could not tell me," said Teddy. "Secret agents must keep their missions secret even from each other. All I know is that two weeks ago, I was asked to fly behind enemy lines to a location in Normandy, France, to pick her up."

"Fly behind enemy lines?" said Jack.

"Yes. I have done that many times," said Teddy. "But when I arrived at the meeting place, she was not waiting for me. I was frantic, and then yesterday I received a message from her, delivered by a French carrier pigeon."

"So she's okay?" asked Annie.

"Well, at least I know she is alive," said Teddy. "The problem is—she wrote her message in a code, in case it fell into enemy hands. But I have had no success trying to make sense of certain parts of it." He pulled a small piece of paper from his pocket and read Kathleen's message aloud:

> Come to me in the darkest time.
> A wand I need, and a magic rhyme.
> Three miles east of Sir Kay's grave,
> Cross a river to find a cave.
> Look for knights, and small, round cows—
> A crack in a rock beneath the boughs.

Teddy sighed. "You see why I cannot share this with anyone in the SOE?" he said. "Even if they could decipher the code, others would not understand her request for the wand and magic rhyme."

"But why *does* she need them?" asked Jack. "Her magic is amazing. Remember when she turned us all into seals?"

"Yes, but these are very, very dark times," said Teddy. "I am not surprised that she may need extra magic. I have found my own powers very limited. That is why I sent for you."

"So . . . do you have something we can take to Kathleen?" asked Jack.

"Oh, yes," said Teddy. "I have the Wand of Dianthus and the rhyme to unlock its magic."

"Great!" said Annie.

"The next two lines of her message I *do* understand," said Teddy. He read on:

> Three miles east of Sir Kay's grave,
> Cross a river to find a cave.

"The secret burial places of Arthur's knights are revealed in one of Merlin's books," said Teddy. "Kathleen knew I would know that the burial place for Sir Kay is Caen, a town in Normandy, France."

"Wait, I'd better write this down," said Jack. He pulled his notebook and pencil out of his backpack. "Spell that, please?"

"C-A-E-N," said Teddy. Jack wrote the town's name in his notebook.

"So we go to Caen," said Annie. "We travel

three miles east, cross a river, and look for a cave."

"Yes," said Teddy. "But I cannot imagine what the next two lines could mean." He read from the note:

> Look for knights and small, round cows—
> A crack in a rock beneath the boughs.

Teddy looked up. "Do you understand this?"

"Not really," said Jack. "There weren't any knights fighting in World War Two."

"Indeed not," said Teddy. "And small, round cows? A crack in a rock? Boughs? What does all that mean?" He folded the note and handed it to Annie. "Well, I trust you to figure this out. I know you are expert decoders."

"You're kidding," said Jack. "Us?"

"Of course," said Teddy. "When Kathleen and I went with you to New York City, you figured out the secret poem to free the unicorn from the museum tapestry, remember? And Morgan's missions for you were often written as riddles."

"Yes, but—" started Jack.

"We have to find Kathleen," said Teddy. "I cannot lose her. So many people have been lost in this war. It really is the darkest time—truly a terrible time."

"It's okay, Teddy," Annie said. "We'll help you."

"Of course we will," said Jack. "We'll do our best."

Teddy took a deep breath, then smiled. "Thank you, my friends," he said. "I am most grateful, and sorry that I cannot be with you in France."

"You're not coming with us?" Jack asked.

"No, tonight the SOE is sending me on an urgent mission to rescue downed airmen in Holland and Belgium," said Teddy. "I must do so before daylight."

"Wow," said Annie.

"It is the sort of thing the SOE does every day," said Teddy. Then he clapped his hands together. "All right! Let us roll up our sleeves and get moving! It is time you put on your parachutes."

"Parachutes?" said Jack.

"Yes!" said Teddy. "You cannot jump from

a plane without parachutes!" He picked up his duffel bag and strode off.

"Wait, did he say we're going to jump from a *plane*?" Jack asked Annie.

"He did," said Annie. "But don't worry, he said he'd give us some magic." She hurried after Teddy.

"I know. But—" began Jack.

"Come along, Jack!" Teddy called to him. "The moon is rising over Glastonbury Tor!"

THREE

Spy Taxi

A full moon glowed over Glastonbury Tor as Jack and Annie followed Teddy between the hedges. Moon shadows stretched along the ground.

Teddy rounded a tall bush at the edge of the abbey grounds. "There she is!" he said. He pointed to a small plane sitting in an open field.

"Oh, man," said Jack. "Is that real?" He thought the tiny plane looked like a cartoon. A single propeller was attached to its rounded nose, and it had big, clunky tires.

"Yes! We call it a spy taxi," said Teddy. "It was made especially for secret operations. It can fly low under enemy radar and land in tight places."

"How many people does it carry?" asked Jack.

"It is designed to carry only a pilot and one passenger," said Teddy. "But it also has room for supply canisters, which I am not carrying. So one of you can take that space."

"But what about when we add Kathleen?" said Annie.

"Do not worry," said Teddy. "I think we can all squeeze together. And if that does not work, perhaps with the magic you bring her, Kathleen can make everyone fit."

"Good," said Jack. He was eager to get the Wand of Dianthus from Teddy. "And another question: where will you pick us up?"

"In the same place I drop you off," said Teddy. "I have been to that drop zone before. It is a lonely field and, to the best of our knowledge, not under enemy observation. You will have to get back there from wherever you find Kathleen."

"Got it," said Annie.

"But an equally important question is *when* I will pick you up," said Teddy. "And that is a question *you* will have to answer."

"How do we answer it?" asked Annie.

"When you know that it is time to leave, you must send me a secret message," said Teddy.

"By pigeon?" asked Annie.

"No, a carrier pigeon might be difficult for you to find. It would be easier to send a message over a wireless radio," said Teddy.

"What should our message say?" asked Annie.

"In your message, say . . ." Teddy thought for a moment, and then smiled. "Say, *The unicorn is free.* And—"

"Wait, wait," said Jack. He wrote in his notebook:

The unicorn is free.

"And then add the date and time," said Teddy. "Send that message over a wireless radio, and

I will pick you up at that time in the field where I drop you tonight."

"How do we find a wireless radio?" asked Jack.

"As you go about your mission, be on the lookout for members of the French Resistance," said Teddy. "Any one of them will help you find a wireless."

"What's the French Resistance?" asked Annie.

"Throughout France, there are French citizens who are secretly fighting back against the Nazis who have occupied their country," Teddy explained. "They are called Resistance fighters. They live very dangerous lives. If a member of the Resistance is caught by the Nazis, he or she will be imprisoned or killed."

"That's terrible," said Annie. "So how do we find someone in the French Resistance?"

"There are many ways," said Teddy. "The simplest way, though, is to make the *V Is for Victory* sign." He held up two fingers in the shape of a V. "It is a secret way for one Resistance fighter to recognize another. You can make the sign with your fingers, draw it on a piece of paper, scratch it into the dirt, or signal any way you can."

Jack and Annie both held fingers up in a *V Is for Victory* sign.

"Good. But be very careful," said Teddy. "If you give the sign to the wrong person, you could end up in the hands of the enemy."

Teddy reached into his large duffel bag and took out some clothes. "These are your disguises," he said. He handed Jack and Annie each a pair of corduroy overalls and a long-sleeved shirt. They pulled them on over their shorts and T-shirts.

"And these," said Teddy. He handed them each a pair of boots. They took off their sneakers and pulled on their boots.

"And a field pack instead of your backpack," said Teddy. He gave Jack an old-fashioned-looking pack with buckles. "You will have to wear it on your chest. Your parachute will be on your back."

Jack moved his notebook, pen, and pencil from his backpack into the field pack. He left his backpack beside his sneakers.

"And now your flying gear," said Teddy. He took out two leather helmets and two pairs of goggles.

Jack and Annie each pulled on a tight-fitting leather helmet. Then Jack positioned his goggles over his glasses.

"And a torchlight," said Teddy. He handed a large, heavy flashlight to Jack.

Jack put the flashlight into the field pack.

"And now . . ." Teddy climbed up a short stepladder to the door of the plane and pulled out two bulky contraptions. They looked like long canvas backpacks attached to a complicated web of straps and buckles. "Your parachute harnesses!" he said, descending the stepladder. "Come on, I will strap you in!"

One at a time, Teddy buckled Jack and Annie into their parachutes. Then he attached the field pack to the front of Jack's harness.

"So how does all this work?" said Jack. He was fighting to stay calm.

Teddy pointed to a large metal ring on the strap across Jack's chest. "This is your rip-cord handle.

When you pull it, it will release your parachute."

"Okay. But *when* do we pull it?" asked Jack.

"After you step off the plane, you will plunge through the open air," said Teddy. "Count to five, then pull hard on the handle. Easy."

Easy? Jack felt a little sick already.

"Remember, jump quickly, one after the other," Teddy said. "If you do not, you will land too far apart and lose each other completely."

"Got it," said Annie.

"And finally . . . ," said Teddy. He handed them each a printed card with a small photograph. "Identity cards. You now have French names—Jean and Aimée."

"Where did you get our photos?" asked Jack.

"A tap of the wand helped with that," said Teddy.

"Cool," said Jack. He was relieved when he remembered they would have the Wand of Dianthus. He thought their mission would be impossible without magic.

"Climb aboard!" said Teddy. He scrambled up the stepladder. Annie bounded after him.

Jack didn't know how she did it. The parachute equipment felt very heavy and clumsy to him. He climbed awkwardly into the plane after Teddy and Annie.

Teddy was already sitting in the pilot's seat, in front of a control panel. "Position yourselves behind me," he said.

Jack and Annie crouched in the narrow space behind the pilot's seat, squashed by their parachute gear.

"Remember, when you jump, face the earth," said Teddy. "Arch your back, spread your arms out, and count to five. Then pull the rip-cord handle. As you float down, keep your elbows close in. Then roll onto your left side."

"Wait, wait," said Jack. "Can you go over all that again?"

"Easy," said Teddy. "Eight simple steps—"

"Hold on, I'll write them down," said Jack. He pulled out his notebook and pencil from the field pack. As Teddy gave the directions again, Jack wrote:

1. Legs together
2. Face earth
3. Arch back
4. Spread arms
5. Count to five
6. Pull rip cord
7. Elbows in
8. Roll to the left

Annie and Jack stared at the notebook, whispering the steps to themselves.

"Got it," said Annie.

"After you land," said Teddy, "roll up your chutes and hide them. Hide your helmets and goggles, too, and destroy your notes."

"Got it," said Annie.

"All right!" said Teddy. "Gas! Oil!"

Jack peered around Teddy at the instrument panel. There were at least a dozen round gauges. Some monitored oil pressure, fuel pressure, and temperature. There were also compasses, brake controls, knobs, buttons, switches, and levers.

Oh, man, thought Jack. "You must have had a lot of training," he said to Teddy.

"Indeed. A full week," said Teddy.

"A *week*? That's *all*?" said Jack.

"Yes, it was very intense," said Teddy as he started flipping switches. "They said I was a natural." Green lights lit up the panel. Needles swung right and left.

"Air intake control!" Teddy announced. He turned a knob. "It is much easier than learning magic!"

Jack felt a wave of panic. "Teddy, slow down!" he said.

"Engine-starter button!" Teddy shouted, pushing a button.

"Teddy, are you sure you know how to do this?" Jack said. But his voice was drowned out by the sound of the engine as the propeller started to spin.

The big wheels began rolling. The plane shook as it bumped over the grass. Then, rocking from side to side, the spy taxi lifted into the air. As the tiny, cramped plane climbed higher into the moonlit night, Teddy pushed more buttons and pulled more levers and shouted out more information.

His heart racing, Jack tried to focus on the eight steps. He whispered: "Legs together—face earth—arch back—spread arms—count to five—pull rip cord—elbows in—roll to the left . . . What does that mean?"

Jack shook Annie's arm. "What does number eight mean?" he shouted.

"What?" she yelled back.

"NUMBER EIGHT!" shouted Jack, jabbing his finger at the list. "DO YOU ROLL IN THE AIR OR ROLL ON THE GROUND?"

"I THINK ON THE GROUND!" Annie answered.

Jack nodded. That made sense. As the plane rumbled through the night, Jack whispered the instructions to himself again and again.

"We are crossing the English Channel!" Teddy called. "Normandy soon, and your dropping point! Get ready!"

Jack crammed his notebook and pencil back into his field pack. His fingers were trembling so much, he had trouble buckling it.

"We are over France now!" shouted Teddy.

"Oh, no," murmured Jack.

"We are coming to the drop zone!" cried Teddy. "Get ready to jump!"

Jack froze with fear.

"Open the door!" yelled Teddy.

Jack couldn't move. Annie pulled up the latch, slid open the door, and crouched at the edge of the plane. With the door open, the roar of the engine and propellers was deafening.

Jack looked down at the endless dark. *No way I can jump!* he thought. *Not without magic help.* Jack bolted upright. *Oh, no! We forgot to get the wand!*

"TEDDY, WE NEED—" Jack shouted.

Teddy couldn't hear him. "JUMP!" he yelled.

"WAIT! MAGIC FOR KATHLEEN!" cried Jack.

It was too late. Annie leaned out of the plane.

She fell forward, arching her back and spreading out her arms.

"TEDDY! THE MAGIC!" cried Jack.

"JUMP, JACK!" Teddy yelled.

Jack had no choice. He had to jump *now,* or he'd land far away from Annie and they'd never find each other. Jack closed his eyes and hurled himself out of the plane, down into the moonlit, windless night.

FOUR

Behind Enemy Lines

Falling through the air, Jack forgot everything he'd written down. He forgot: *legs together—face earth—arch back—spread arms—count to five.* But miraculously, he remembered, *Pull rip cord*!

Jack fumbled for the cord on his chest strap. He grabbed the metal ring and pulled hard. The parachute popped out from Jack's harness.

As the chute's white canopy opened above Jack, it yanked him backward. The billowing silk slowed his downward plunge. Jack clutched his field pack as he drifted through the night air.

The drone of the spy taxi engine faded into the distance. Teddy was gone. Not far away, Jack could see Annie in the moonlight, floating to earth, too. "Hi!" she yelled to Jack.

Jack was too amazed to answer. He was filled with a strange happiness as they both drifted in a dreamlike fall toward the field below.

Suddenly the earth rose up to meet him. Jack hit the ground with a thud and, remembering the eighth step, rolled onto his left side. He lay in the cold damp grass, trying to catch his breath.

"We're in France! We did it!" Annie called from nearby. She threw off her parachute harness and ran to Jack.

"We did it," he repeated, sitting up. His parachute lay spread on the ground behind him. "We did it!"

"Wasn't it fun?" said Annie.

"Yeah . . . yeah, it was," said Jack in a daze.

Jack wiggled out of his harness. Floating through the night sky actually *had* been fun—

"Suddenly the earth rose up to meet him."

although he had no idea how he'd done what he'd just done. "I have some bad news, though."

"What?" asked Annie.

"Teddy forgot to give us the magic wand for Kathleen," said Jack.

"Oh, no," moaned Annie.

"'Oh, no' is right," said Jack.

"I guess it means we'll have to help Kathleen without magic," said Annie. "But that's okay. We have lots of skills."

"Like what?" Jack asked.

"Well, like—just a lot of skills," said Annie. "Don't worry. We can do this. Let's go."

"Hold on. We have to roll up our chutes and figure out where we are first," said Jack. He and Annie looked around. In the moonlight, they could see trees bordering the field on three sides and a road on the fourth side. A church with a tall white steeple was down the road.

"Let's take that road," said Annie.

"Yep," said Jack. "That should work. But we

have to hide the parachutes before we go."

In the quiet night, Jack stood up and strapped his field pack on his back. He and Annie carefully rolled up the soft silk canopies of their parachutes. They gathered the straps and tangled cords in their arms and started across the field.

"Hey," said Annie, stopping. "I hear a plane."

"Teddy's back!" said Jack. "He remembered that he forgot to give us the magic wand and spell!"

"Yay!" said Annie.

"Wait," said Jack, squinting at the sky. Not just one plane—but *three* planes droned overhead!

"It's not Teddy," said Annie.

"Run!" said Jack.

As the planes dipped down over the field, Jack and Annie ran toward the road, lugging the bundles of their parachutes.

"Get down!" Jack shouted. He pushed Annie into a ditch at the edge of the road. Clutching their gear, they lay in a thick bed of wet and rotting leaves.

The planes roared off into the distance. After a long silence, Jack and Annie stood up. "They're gone," Jack said.

"So what do we do now?" Annie asked.

"We have to find that town," said Jack. He looked around at the moonlit dark. "But we might have to wait for daylight to figure out how to get there."

Jack saw the glare of car headlights coming up the road. "Hide!" cried Annie.

They threw themselves facedown again in the ditch. Jack held his breath as the car rumbled by. Soon all was quiet again, except for the distant barking of dogs.

Jack and Annie lifted their heads. "We have to get away from this road," said Jack, "and find a place where we can stay hidden for a while. Remember, we're behind enemy lines. Nazis could be anywhere. Come on."

Annie didn't say anything. She didn't move.

"Hey, are you okay?" Jack asked her.

"No. I'm scared," Annie said in a whisper.

"You are?" said Jack. He knelt beside her. Annie was never scared. *He* was always the scared one.

"This seems so dangerous," she said. "Hiding from Nazis."

Jack was frightened, too. She was right. Hiding from Nazis seemed much scarier than anything they'd done before. But if Annie was scared, *he* had to act brave. "It's okay," he said. "Think about what you told me earlier—we don't have magic, but we've got skills. And we've used our skills again and again on our missions. Right?"

"Right . . . ," said Annie.

"Well, we'll use them this time," said Jack.

"You think we can?" asked Annie.

"I know we can," said Jack. "First, we need to get to a safe spot." He pulled out his flashlight and pointed it toward the road. The light lit up a sign that said *Biéville.* Not far down the road was the white church. "Okay. Biéville. This is where Teddy will pick us up with Kathleen."

"Right," said Annie. "The field near the sign that says Biéville, near the white church."

"See, we solved that. With our observation skill," said Jack. "So now we'll head into the woods across the road and hide there until daylight. Okay? That's the skill of, um—"

"Being smart," said Annie. She stood up. "Let's bury our stuff here."

"Good idea, I'd forgotten that," said Jack. "See? Skills! We got 'em!"

They buried their parachute gear under piles of leaves and brush. "Don't forget these," said Jack. He pulled off his helmet and goggles and shoved them under the heap. Annie did the same. "And my notes!" Jack ripped his notes out of his notebook, tore them up, and hid the pieces with everything else.

"Okay!" he said. "Onward! Let's go!" With Annie close behind, Jack led the way across the road and into the woods.

Tramping through tangled undergrowth, Jack and Annie made their way deeper into the moonlit forest. They didn't stop until they came to a wooden fence. When Jack pointed their flashlight toward the area beyond the fence, it shone on neat rows of vine-covered trellises.

"Looks like a vineyard," he said.

"What's that?" asked Annie.

"You know, where they grow grapes to make wine," said Jack. "We shouldn't trespass—"

Before he could finish, Annie grabbed his arm. "Listen!"

Jack listened. From the woods behind them came the sound of a dog barking. Then he heard men's voices.

"They're searching for us!" said Annie.

"Trespass!" said Jack. He turned off his flashlight, and they scrambled over the wooden fence and took off running through the moonlit vineyard. They ran between long rows of grapevines until they saw a small farmhouse ahead. Smoke was rising from the chimney. Not far from the house was a barn.

The barking behind them was getting louder. It sounded as if the searchers had entered the vineyard and were heading their way.

"There!" said Jack. He grabbed Annie's hand and pulled her toward the barn. Jack yanked open a wooden door, and the two of them ran inside.

Jack switched his flashlight back on and shined it around the barn. Horses stood in stalls, swishing their tails and munching hay.

"There!" Annie pointed to a stack of hay bales in the back. They crouched together behind the bales. Jack turned off the flashlight and put it in his field pack. He and Annie waited motionless, huddled on the floor, inhaling hay dust and animal smells and trying to breathe as quietly as they could.

The barking grew louder and closer. The horses moved restlessly. Jack heard men shouting above the barking, but he couldn't understand what they were saying.

Then the door to the barn banged open. "Fritz! Check inside!" a man said.

Jack heard two sharp barks and the sound of a dog sniffing and scratching. The next thing he knew, a German shepherd bounded over to the hay bales! With a low growl, it bared its teeth.

"It's okay!" Annie whispered to the dog. "It's okay."

The dog snorted and sniffed their faces. Jack didn't move a muscle as Annie gently stroked the dog's head and whispered in its ear.

The dog grew calm. Annie whispered again. The shepherd licked her face. Then it barked once and loped out of the barn.

"Nothing in there, Fritz?" the man said to the dog. "Good boy." Then the door slammed shut. The men's voices faded away. Everything grew quiet.

Jack and Annie waited a long moment. Then Jack let out his breath. "What did you say to that police dog?" he asked.

Annie shrugged. "I said, 'Good dog, everything's okay. We're friends.' I just didn't tell him whose friends we were."

Jack shook his head in amazement.

"Let's escape while we can," said Annie.

Jack was relieved. Annie sounded like her old self again. *Calming the dog calmed her, too,* he thought. "Okay, but let's go slowly."

Just as Jack and Annie stood up, the door to the barn creaked open again. Jack's heart pounded as they dropped back behind the hay bales.

The barn was lit with flickering lantern light. Jack heard footsteps on the wooden floor. The steps grew closer and closer. Then a man with a black beard peered over the hay bales. He wore a black beret slanted over one eye.

"Aha! We found you!" he said in a deep, growly whisper.

FIVE

Resistance

Jack was too terrified to speak.

Annie slowly held up two fingers in a *V Is for Victory* sign.

What is she doing? Jack thought wildly. *We don't know who this guy is!*

The man glared at Annie for a moment; then his craggy face broke into a smile, and he held up his fingers in a matching V.

Oh, man, thought Jack. *Did we really just find a member of the French Resistance?*

"Who are they, Gaston?" a woman called from the barn doorway.

"Who are you?" Gaston asked in a raspy voice.

"J-J . . . ," Jack stuttered, terrified.

"Jean and Aimée," Annie said quickly.

Annie's a good spy, Jack thought. He'd completely forgotten their French names.

"Really?" said the man. "Are those your real names?"

Annie laughed. "No, our real names are Jack and Annie."

Oh, brother, Jack thought. *She's a terrible spy!*

"And what are Jack and Annie doing in our barn?" asked Gaston.

"We're hiding from the Nazis," Annie said.

"Well, then," said Gaston, "you are in the right place."

"For the moment, you are safe, children," said the woman, stepping forward. She wore a shawl around her shoulders and a kerchief over her dark hair. "Hello, my dears. My name is Suzette, and this is my husband, Gaston."

"Nice to meet you," said Annie.

"Come with us, back to our house," said Suzette.

Jack and Annie climbed out from behind the hay bales and followed the French couple to the door of the barn. Before they left, Gaston blew out his lantern light. "Silence," he ordered, "until we get into the house."

Gaston and Suzette led Jack and Annie through the dark to the front door of the small stone farmhouse. Once they were inside, Jack and Annie looked around the room. It had a low ceiling. Candles burned on a heavy wooden table. A fire flickered in a large fireplace.

Suzette placed an iron bar over the front door, while Gaston closed the window shutters.

"Sit, children," said Suzette. "We will have apple cider, and you will share our dinner."

Jack and Annie sat at the table near the hearth. A pot hung over the fire. Jack relaxed a little as he smelled roasting potatoes, onions, and carrots.

Gaston poured cider into mugs, and Suzette

prepared four bowls of stew. Then the couple joined Jack and Annie at the table. The fire crackled as they all quietly sipped cider and ate their dinner.

When they were finished, Gaston leaned back in his chair and lit a pipe. "You know," he said, "when the Nazis were here earlier, they were not looking for you."

"They weren't?" said Annie.

"No, they were looking for two paratroopers who'd been spotted dropping into a field near here," said Gaston.

"Oh. Then they *were* looking for us," said Jack.

"No, no—" Gaston stopped and gave Jack a funny look. "Unless you two could be those paratroopers?"

"Yes, we could be," said Annie.

"But no!" said Gaston. "How could two *children* parachute into Normandy? And why?"

"We're working with agents of the SOE," said Annie.

"But no!" Gaston said again.

"Oh, my," said Suzette. "Are things so bad that children are being recruited as spies now?"

"Well, not just *any* children," said Annie. "We were asked because one of our best friends is an SOE agent. We have information that she is three miles east of Caen. We're supposed to find her and get her out of France."

"Then you do not have far to go," said Gaston. "We are only four miles northwest of Caen."

"There is great danger, though," said Suzette. "The city is surrounded by Nazi patrols. You will need the right papers."

"We have identity cards," said Annie.

"Good," said Gaston, standing up. "Come with me. We will hide you here tonight and help you get on your way in the morning."

"Thank you," said Jack, standing up with Annie.

"Thanks for the dinner," Annie said to Suzette.

"It is my pleasure to feed two brave children again," Suzette said.

Why did she say "again"? Jack wondered.

"Come along," Gaston said, waving his arm. Jack and Annie followed him to a room off the kitchen.

Gaston pulled aside a floor rug, revealing a trapdoor. He lifted the door, and then, carrying a lantern, he led Jack and Annie down a staircase to a cellar. Hundreds of wine bottles sat in racks along the walls of the dank, musty room.

"Suzette will bring bedding," said Gaston. "And you can keep the light with you." He placed the lantern on a long table and then started back up the steps. Without looking back, he raised his hand. "Good night!" he said.

"Thank you!" called Jack and Annie.

When Gaston was gone, Annie sat down at the table. "Wow, they saved us," she said.

"For now," said Jack.

"I wonder what these little rubber blocks are for," said Annie. She picked up a small block from the table and held it to the lantern light. "Look—it has the letter *H* on it."

Jack walked over to her. On the table were dozens

of small rubber blocks and several stacks of paper.

"And this one has the letter *S*," said Annie, holding up another block.

"Here's a *D*," said Jack. "*S* and *U*. They're all letters. It must be a printing set."

"Check this out," said Annie. She picked up a piece of paper from one of the stacks on the table. She showed it to Jack.

He read the print on the page aloud:

HOPE AND COURAGE!
FREEDOM SOON!

Annie thumbed through more papers in the stack. "They all say the same thing," she said. "It's a bunch of flyers. Do you think Gaston and Suzette secretly pass them out?"

"Here is your bedding, children," said Suzette, coming down the steps to the cellar. When she saw Annie holding one of the flyers, she stopped.

"Did you and Gaston print these?" Annie asked.

Suzette crossed the room and stood in the

lantern light. "No, we didn't," she said softly. "Our sons did."

"Your sons?" asked Annie.

"Our brave twins, Tom and Theo," said Suzette. "They are couriers for the French Resistance."

"What are couriers?" asked Jack.

"Couriers travel on bicycles, delivering messages from one resistance group to another," said Suzette. "Tom and Theo also printed flyers to give people hope. On their courier routes, they sometimes posted them when no one was looking. Only . . . one day someone *was* looking."

"What happened?" asked Annie.

"Three months ago we received word that Tom and Theo were picked up in Paris by the Nazis," said Suzette.

"So . . . they're in prison now?" asked Annie.

Suzette took a deep breath. "We do not know what has happened to them," she said.

"I'm sorry," said Annie. "Are Tom and Theo children?"

"They are young men. Twenty-two years old,"

said Suzette. "But they will always be our children."

"Are you and Gaston in the French Resistance, too?" asked Jack.

Suzette nodded. "Our job is to gather and send information." She turned away from them. "But *now* my job is to make your beds."

"We'll help," said Annie. She and Jack helped Suzette spread the threadbare blankets on the floor.

"I fear you will not be so comfortable," said Suzette. "But at least you will be safe."

"That's all that matters," said Jack.

"Thank you, Suzette!" said Annie, and she hugged the kind Frenchwoman.

"Try to sleep now, children," said Suzette. "You will need all your strength tomorrow to find your friend." Then she climbed the stairs and closed the door to the cellar.

"That's so sad about their boys," said Annie.

"Yeah," said Jack. He didn't know what else to say. He was amazed by the courage of Gaston and Suzette. Even after their sons were caught, the couple was willing to risk their lives to help others.

"So tomorrow we head to Caen," said Annie.

Jack nodded. "Do you have Kathleen's message?"

Annie pulled the piece of paper from her pocket and read aloud:

Come to me in the darkest time.
A wand I need, and a magic rhyme.
Three miles east of Sir Kay's grave,
Cross a river to find a cave.
Look for knights, and small, round cows—
A crack in a rock beneath the boughs.

"So we've figured out the first four lines," said Annie. "We know Kathleen needs magic—which Teddy forgot to give us."

"Right," said Jack. "And we know we have to go three miles east of a town named Caen—and then cross a river to find a cave."

"Right," said Annie. "And then the weird part." She reread:

Look for knights, and small, round cows—
A crack in a rock beneath the boughs.

Jack shook his head. His brain was getting foggy. "Let's ask Gaston and Suzette in the morning if they have any ideas," he said.

"Good plan," said Annie.

They pulled off their boots and lay down on the ragged blankets.

"We'll figure it all out tomorrow," Annie murmured.

"Yeah, right now, I'm way too tired," said Jack, closing his eyes. He was exhausted from traveling through time to Glastonbury, flying over the English Channel, parachuting into Normandy, running from planes, lying in a ditch, hiding in a barn, escaping Nazis, and making friends with people in the French Resistance—all between twilight and bedtime.

SIX

THE HOUR OF BATTLE

"Jack! Annie! Wake up!" said Suzette. She stood at the bottom of the cellar stairs. "It is morning. There is news!"

Jack opened his eyes. Where were they? He squinted at the racks of wine bottles against the wall and the table with the flyers and the printing set. Then he remembered: a cellar in Normandy, France. He sat up.

"What news?" Annie asked.

"We just received a message from the London BBC," said Suzette. "It was the message we have been waiting for. The hour of the great battle is coming! Tomorrow, June sixth."

"What battle?" asked Jack.

"The invasion of France," said Suzette. "The invasion by the Allies. The English, Scots, Americans, Canadians, and others will all invade France and drive out the Nazis, starting tomorrow!"

"Really?" said Jack.

"Yes!" said Suzette. "Excuse me, I must get back to Gaston. He is getting more news from the BBC over the wireless." She hurried up the steps.

"Oh, wow!" said Annie. "Did you hear what she said?"

"Yes, the Allies—" said Jack.

"No, the *wireless*—" interrupted Annie. "They have a wireless! Once we find Kathleen, we can come back here and send Teddy a message."

"You're right," said Jack. "But now let's go find out more about that invasion."

Jack and Annie dashed up the stairs, taking two steps at a time. Gaston was at the kitchen table. Smoking his pipe, he was hunched over a small open suitcase. Inside was a radio with tubes and knobs. Gaston wore a headset and was listening carefully.

"Plan Purple!" he shouted.

"Plan Purple!" Suzette repeated.

"Plan Purple? What's that?" Jack said.

"It means all the Resistance must act now," she said. "They must destroy communication lines to keep the Nazis in the south from finding out about the invasion."

Gaston took off his headset and pointed his pipe at Suzette. "Plan Green—and now Plan Purple."

"What's Plan Green?" said Jack.

"We received word of Plan Green a few days ago," said Suzette. "It called upon Resistance fighters to blow up bridges and train tracks to keep enemy troops from traveling here."

"Why would they travel *here*?" asked Annie.

"This is where the Allied invasion will take place," said Gaston. "Here in Normandy! The Allies will come by air and sea. Tomorrow they will land on beaches not far from Caen, and then fight their way across France."

"Oh, man. I get it now," Jack murmured. "*D-Day.* Tomorrow is D-Day."

"Listen to me, children," said Gaston. He pointed his pipe at them. "You must tell *no one* what we have just told you."

"We won't. We promise," said Annie, shaking her head.

"And you must leave France at once," Gaston said. "Now!"

"Leave now?" said Jack.

"Yes, return to England immediately," said Gaston. "There will be terrible fighting here tomorrow. Many bombs will drop."

"But we have to find our friend Kathleen," said Annie.

"Ahh! You cannot worry about your friend now!" Gaston said. "You must worry about yourselves!"

"It is quite possible, children, that your friend has already gone south," Suzette said. "Perhaps she has crossed the Pyrenees mountains into Spain. Many people have escaped that way and found safety."

"Gaston was at the kitchen table."

"We have to at least *try* to find Kathleen before we can leave," said Annie. "That's our mission."

"Then you have only today to find her," said Gaston. "You *must* leave France by nightfall."

"We'd better get going, then," Annie said.

"Wait," said Jack. He turned to Gaston. "We have a favor to ask. Can you send a message by wireless to our contact in the SOE and let him know that we must be picked up tonight?"

"Yes, I can do that," said Gaston.

"And I will prepare food for you," said Suzette.

"And I'll get our stuff," said Annie.

Suzette and Annie left the kitchen. Gaston grabbed a piece of paper and a pencil. "What should the message say?" he asked Jack.

"The unicorn is free—nightfall June fifth," said Jack.

"The unicorn . . . is . . . free . . . nightfall . . . June fifth," Gaston repeated as he wrote down the message. "I like that," he said, nodding. "The unicorn is free. It sounds very hopeful. It sounds like a message I would like to get about my sons someday."

"I'm sorry they disappeared," Jack said.

"Yes . . . ," whispered Gaston. "As am I." He shook his head. "Well!" His voice boomed. "It's wartime! And war is terrible for everyone, is it not?"

"Yes, it is," said Jack.

"Got everything!" said Annie, returning to the kitchen. She was carrying their boots and Jack's field pack.

"And here is a bit of food," said Suzette. She gave Annie a small sack.

"Thanks!" said Annie. She put the sack of food in Jack's pack. Then she and Jack pulled on their boots.

"It is half past eight now," said Gaston, looking at his watch. "It will be dark by eight o'clock tonight. So you have nearly twelve hours to find your friend."

"Oh, we almost forgot to ask you!" said Annie. She pulled out Kathleen's rhyme. "This is the message she sent about where to look for her." She read aloud the third and fourth lines of the rhyme:

Three miles east of Sir Kay's grave,
Cross a river to find a cave.

"So we know we go to Caen first," said Jack, "since that's where Sir Kay is buried. And then we'll head three miles east from there and cross a river."

"The River Orne!" said Suzette.

"Great!" said Jack. "And then we look for a cave."

"Yes, but there are many caves east of the River Orne in Mondeville," said Gaston. "Long ago, they mined limestone rock in that area, creating caverns and tunnels."

"I wonder how we find the right one," Jack said.

"I do not know," said Gaston, frowning.

"Here are the next lines," said Annie. She showed Gaston the message and read aloud:

Look for knights, and small, round cows—
A crack in a rock beneath the boughs.

"Knights?" growled Gaston. "What does your

friend mean? Knights in armor? Knights from the Middle Ages?"

Annie shrugged.

"Small, round cows . . . ?" said Suzette. She shook her head. "That doesn't make sense to me."

"Nor to me," said Gaston.

"It's okay. We'll figure out that part later," said Annie. "You've been a big help just telling us about the River Orne and the caves in Mondeville." She put the note back in her pocket.

"Let's go," said Jack. He took his field pack from Annie and pulled it on.

"Come along, then," said Gaston. He led them out of the farmhouse into the chilly morning. The windy air smelled of wood smoke. The sky was overcast.

"Do you have money?" said Suzette.

"Actually, no," said Jack.

"Gaston?" said Suzette.

Gaston reached into the pocket of his trousers and brought out a handful of coins. "French francs for you," he said, handing them to Jack.

"Thank you!" Jack dropped the francs into his pocket.

"Gaston, they will need bicycles, too," said Suzette.

"Yes, yes. Come along," said Gaston. They all followed him to the barn. Gaston stepped inside and came out a moment later, carrying two bikes. "You can ride these. They belonged to our boys when they were younger."

"Just follow any road to the south," said Suzette, "and you will come to Caen."

"Keep to the back roads," said Gaston. "There are fewer motorcars on them."

"Which way is south?" asked Annie.

"Wait, I will give you something to guide you." Suzette slipped back into the house and returned a moment later. "Take this compass. It belonged to Tom and Theo." She handed a small silver compass to Annie. Then she gave Jack and Annie each a flat black cap. "These berets belonged to them, too."

"Thank you," said Annie. When they put on the

berets, Jack adjusted his to look like Gaston's.

Suzette smiled. "Good. Now you look French."

"If you come to a checkpoint," said Gaston, "act very calm when you pass the sentries. If they stop you and ask for papers, show them your identity cards. Do not give the V sign to anyone unless you are certain that person is on our side."

"Many of our citizens do not belong to the Resistance," Suzette explained.

"In these times, you never know who your friends and enemies are," growled Gaston. "And that is why you must tell no one about the invasion tomorrow."

"We won't, we promise," said Annie.

"But I'll tell *you* guys something," said Jack.

"What is that?" said Gaston.

Jack took a deep breath, and then said, "The invasion will be a success. Tom and Theo wrote the truth: France *will* gain back its freedom."

Gaston gave him a crooked smile.

"Jack's right," said Annie. "It might take time, but we know you'll be free. We know it for a fact."

Sudden tears filled Gaston's eyes. He nodded briskly, and then turned his face away.

"Thank you for your kind words, children," said Suzette, putting an arm around Gaston. "Ride south on the lane running past the farm. Gaston will send your message over the wireless. I hope your SOE contact receives it. And I hope you find your dear friend and take her back to England with you."

"Thanks," said Jack. "Thanks for everything."

Jack and Annie climbed onto the bikes. They rode down the bumpy dirt path away from the farmhouse. When they came to the lane, Annie pulled out the compass. "South—that way," she said, pointing to the right.

Before they turned onto the lane, Jack and Annie looked back. The French couple was still watching them. Gaston held up two fingers in a *V Is for Victory* sign.

Jack and Annie each flashed the sign back at him. Then they turned onto the lane and headed south.

SEVEN

Friends and Enemies

Jack and Annie rode with the wind at their backs. The spring air smelled of plowed soil and freshly cut hay. As their bicycles wobbled down the dirt lane, they passed apple orchards, wheat fields, vineyards, and farmhouses.

"I can't believe it!" Jack called to Annie. "The Allied invasion of Normandy! That was called D-Day! D-Day! Have you ever heard of it?"

"Yes, but I don't know exactly what it was," said Annie.

"I read a book about it," said Jack. "It was one

of the most important military events of all time. Over a hundred thousand soldiers landed in Normandy, France, to fight Hitler's army. It was the beginning of the end of World War Two! I can't believe we came here on the day before D-Day."

"I hope everything doesn't get destroyed by bombs," said Annie. "It's beautiful here."

"Yeah, it is," said Jack. The countryside looked like an old painting: peach-colored farmhouses, apple trees with white flowers, red poppies blooming in fields. Everything was so peaceful and lovely that Jack could hardly believe the battle of D-Day would start here tomorrow. It gave him a strange feeling to know what was coming.

After bumping over ruts and ridges, Jack and Annie came to the end of the dirt lane. Annie checked the compass. "Left," she said.

They turned left and pedaled down the wide road bordered by hedgerows. The hedges were so tall it was impossible to see beyond them.

"Are we on a back road?" Annie asked.

"I can't tell," Jack said.

They hadn't gone much farther when a motorcycle turned onto the road and headed their way.

Friend? Enemy? Jack wondered anxiously. In case it was an enemy, he called out to Annie, "Act normal!"

"Right!" said Annie. They both smiled broadly and steered their bikes single file along the edge of the road. Jack was glad that Suzette had said wearing berets made them look French. When the motorcycle roared past, the driver didn't even look their way.

The motorcycle disappeared in the distance, but then another car turned onto the road. As it headed toward them, Jack tried to look normal again. Just as the car sped past, he glanced in its direction. To his amazement, a woman driver flashed a quick *V Is for Victory* sign.

Jack grinned and gave the sign back. "Friend!" he called to Annie. The woman's V signal made him feel hopeful. *Maybe this isn't going to be so hard,* he thought.

Coming toward them next was a horse and cart

driven by a young man who looked like a farmer. Seated beside him was a teenage girl. When they saw Jack and Annie, they smiled and nodded.

Definitely friends, Jack thought. When he got close to the couple, he flashed the *V Is for Victory* sign at them, too.

An angry look crossed the man's face. He cried out in alarm. He pulled his horse to a halt and pointed at Jack and Annie. "Couriers! Resistance!" he shouted.

Oh, no! thought Jack. Gaston was right! In these times, you really didn't know who was a friend and who was an enemy!

Behind the horse and cart, another motorcycle was rumbling down the road. The rider wore a gray uniform. The people in the cart flagged him down.

"GO!" Jack cried.

He and Annie wheeled around and raced their bikes against the wind. When Jack looked back, the motorcycle was coming toward them—fast!

"Ditch the bikes!" Annie shouted. They skidded to a stop, dropped their bikes to the ground, and bolted through an opening in a hedgerow.

Scraped by branches and thorns, they pushed their way through the narrow gap until they burst onto farmland. As they ran through a cow pasture, Jack looked around wildly for a place to hide. "Barn!" he cried, pointing. He and Annie ran toward a red wooden building next to a silo. When they drew closer to the entrance, they saw a man in white clothes putting two large milk cans into the back of a white truck.

"Help!" cried Annie.

The milkman looked startled, but as the motorcycle crashed through the hedge at the edge of the property, he seemed to understand everything at once. "Quick! In the truck!" he shouted.

Jack and Annie scrambled into the back of the truck and found a hiding place behind rows of tall milk canisters. Crouching behind the canisters, they covered their mouths so no one would hear them gasping for breath.

The milkman slammed the back door of the

truck shut. There was a panel between the front seat and the windowless back area. Jack and Annie sat in the dark and listened to the motorcycle thunder closer and then stop. Through the closed door, they could hear bits of conversation from outside:

"Yes . . . two . . . boy and girl." "Resistance couriers . . ." "Yes, you are sure. . . ." "Yes . . . good . . ." "Thank you for your help. . . ."

Moments later, Jack heard the motorcycle rev up and drive away.

The milkman started his engine. Then, with the large canisters jiggling in their crates, the truck began bouncing over the road.

"I guess we're going with him," whispered Annie.

"I wonder if he's a friend or enemy," whispered Jack.

"A friend," said Annie. "He must have told the motorcycle guy we went in the opposite direction."

"*Or* he could be taking us to the police," whispered Jack. "Maybe the motorcycle guy was thanking him for locking us in his truck and taking us to the Nazis."

"Oh, no. I hadn't thought of that," Annie whispered. Clutching their berets, they jiggled with the clattering milk cans as the truck continued on.

After a while, the milk truck stopped again. It sounded like the driver was getting out.

Jack froze. He heard the back door handle click. Then the door swung open. The milkman pulled out a large milk canister and whispered, "All clear! Hurry!"

"Thanks!" said Annie.

Leaving the door open, the milkman carried the canister away from the truck.

"Go!" said Jack.

He and Annie jumped out of the back of the truck. It was parked in front of a long building with a sign that said:

CAEN MILK PROCESSING PLANT

"Look! We're in Caen!" said Annie, pointing to the sign. "Isn't that great?"

"Go! *Go!*" said Jack. He and Annie raced across

a street and headed down a narrow alley.

"Wait," Jack said, stopping in his tracks. "We shouldn't run. It will make us look suspicious." They stopped for a moment and tried to catch their breath.

"The milkman *was* a friend," said Annie.

"Definitely," said Jack. "Okay. Let's go. Act normal."

Jack and Annie stepped out from the alley and into a busy town square. In the middle of the square was an outdoor market. Women with children strolled from booth to booth, buying lettuce, peas, potatoes, flowers, linens, and lace. Surrounding the square were cobblestone streets lined with quaint buildings. There was a church covered with ivy, a small train depot, and a sidewalk café with a red striped awning.

Again, Jack found it difficult to believe that a great battle was about to take place. "This is all going to change tomorrow," he said to Annie as they strolled through the market.

"I know," Annie said. "I wish we could tell everyone to leave today."

"Yep," said Jack. He looked at a clock tower in the square. "It's almost ten. We have ten hours left until nightfall."

"Well, we're in Caen," said Annie. "Now we have to go three miles east to the River Orne and the caves of Mondeville."

"Right," said Jack.

"Excuse me!" Annie called to a young woman pushing a baby buggy. "Can you please tell us how to get to Mondeville?"

"It is very easy," said the woman. "Just a short train ride. You get off at the first stop." She pointed to the depot next to the café.

"Thanks," said Annie.

"You're welcome," said the woman. She waved two fingers and kept pushing the carriage across the square.

"Friend," Annie said to Jack.

"How do you know?" he asked.

"She gave me a *V Is for Victory* sign," said Annie.

"Or maybe she just happened to use two fingers to wave to you," said Jack. "Even though the milkman was a friend, we can never be sure who our friends and enemies are. Remember the farmer and the girl in the cart?"

"Yeah, I didn't see *that* coming," said Annie.

"Not in a million years," said Jack.

"I thought—" said Annie

The roar of engines interrupted her. Four open black cars rolled into the square and parked in a line. Each car had a red, white, and black symbol on the side. Jack recognized it as a swastika, the symbol of the Nazis. Soldiers got out of the cars and stood at the edge of the square, watching the shoppers. They wore gray uniforms with black belts and tall boots.

"Enemies," Jack said under his breath.

"Definitely," said Annie.

EIGHT

The Train

With the arrival of the Nazis, the atmosphere in the square changed. Vendors fell silent. Shoppers lowered their heads and grabbed the hands of their children.

"We should catch that train as soon as possible," said Jack.

"You bet," said Annie. "Look normal."

With their hands in their pockets, Jack and Annie walked as calmly as they could from the market toward the train depot. With quick steps, they crossed the street and entered the small station.

"Tickets," Jack said to Annie. He headed to the ticket window and placed some coins in front of the ticket agent. "Two for Mondeville, please."

The ticket agent counted out some coins, then gave Jack two tickets. "Thank you," said Jack. He and Annie stepped away from the window and walked out to the tracks.

Jack noticed that the waiting passengers were anxiously watching a scene at the end of the station platform. Some Nazi soldiers had stopped an old man. The man had his hands in the air. He looked terrified as the soldiers checked his pockets.

"What are they doing?" Annie asked.

"Don't look," said Jack. He grabbed her hand so she wouldn't hurry to the man's aid.

But he felt fury, too. *Why torment an old man?* he wondered. He wanted to shout at the Nazi soldiers: LEAVE US ALL ALONE! But just like the other bystanders, he was too scared to do anything. He gripped Annie's hand tighter and pulled her in the other direction. "Come on."

To Jack's great relief, he heard the train whistle

blow. Soon the train rounded the bend, puffing steam. The crowd stepped back as the black engine chugged into the station. It let out an ear-piercing shriek and jolted to a stop. Doors slid open and people stepped out onto the platform and headed for the station.

"All aboard!" shouted the conductor, and the waiting passengers moved toward the tracks.

Jack and Annie climbed into one of the rear cars. "Where are our seats?" Annie asked Jack.

"I don't know," he said. He looked at their tickets. "It says 'second-class.' "

"Excuse me, where are the second-class seats?" Annie asked an older woman with a friendly face.

"Follow me." The woman led them up the train corridor and stopped in front of an empty compartment. "You can sit in there," she said, then continued on her way.

Annie and Jack opened a glass door and stepped into a small space with four seats. Jack pulled off his field pack and sat down next to Annie near the window.

"I hate them," said Annie.

Jack knew exactly who she meant.

The whistle blew. The train jolted and began moving. Huffing and puffing, it left the depot and chugged down the tracks away from Caen.

"It's a short ride," said Annie.

"Not short enough," said Jack. "Listen." Even above the roar of the train, he could hear boots stomping down the corridor outside their compartment.

"Ignore them," said Annie.

"Got it," said Jack.

"Oh, Jean! Look! Lovely trees!" Annie pointed out the window.

"Yes, Aimée! They *are* lovely!" exclaimed Jack. "Remember—"

Before he could finish, the door to the compartment slid open. Two Nazi officials stood in the doorway. "Identity papers, please?" one said.

Jack's heart started to pound, but he turned and faked a friendly smile. "Oh! Yes, sure," he said. He pulled out his identity card and showed it to the official. Annie smiled and showed her card, too.

The soldier looked carefully at the cards, then handed them back. "Your bag now," he said to Jack, holding out his hand.

"My pack? Sure," said Jack.

But before he could hand over his field pack, Annie snatched it away from him. "Why do you want it?" she asked the man, grinning.

"I need to look inside it," said the official.

"Really?" said Annie. "There's nothing interesting inside."

Why is she doing this? Jack wondered. He couldn't think of anything in the pack that could get them into trouble—just lunch and Jack's pencil and notebook, with all the notes torn out.

"Give it to me," demanded the official.

Annie didn't move. Her smile had faded, replaced by a look of fear.

What is wrong with her? Jack wondered. He gently pried the field pack loose from her grip. "It's okay," he assured her. "He can look in it."

Grinning crazily, he handed the field pack over to the soldier.

The Nazi unbuckled Jack's pack. He reached in and pulled out the small cloth sack that Suzette had given them. He opened it and took out two apples, a chunk of cheese, and two pieces of black bread. He handed the food to the other official. Then he reached deeper into the field pack and pulled out some papers.

Jack was confused. *Where did those come from?*

The soldier held up one of the papers. It was one of the flyers printed by Tom and Theo!

HOPE AND COURAGE!
FREEDOM SOON!

The soldier put the papers back into the pack. Then he narrowed his eyes at Jack. "So you are working for the other side?"

"What? No!" said Jack. He looked at Annie. "How . . . ?"

"Sorry," Annie whispered. "I wanted to help them. Tom and Theo."

"Stand up!" the official barked at Jack.

"No!" cried Annie. "Please! He didn't do anything! It was me! I did it!"

The Nazi official pushed Annie aside. "Boy, I am placing you under arrest," he said. But just as the man reached out to grab Jack, an explosion rocked the train car.

The sound of screeching brakes split the air. The train ground to a sudden stop. Jack and Annie were thrown from their seats.

The soldiers fell to their hands and knees. Passengers scrambled up the corridor, screaming and yelling: "What happened? What happened?" "Resistance!" "Blew up tracks ahead!"

The two Nazis jumped to their feet. Ignoring Jack and Annie, they hurried away from the compartment.

Jack looked out the window. A few hundred yards in front of the train, black smoke was rising into the air. "Plan Green!" he said. "Let's get out of here!" He grabbed his field pack and started out of the compartment. But more soldiers were running down the corridor, shoving all the passengers aside.

Annie grabbed Jack's arm. "The window!" she cried. "Out! Climb out!"

Jack straddled the window ledge, then swung his leg over and dropped to the embankment below. He reached up and helped Annie drop to the ground, too.

Looking down the tracks, Jack saw train workers and soldiers running toward the billowing black smoke. Sirens were screaming. Passengers were fleeing from all the cars on the train.

"Come on!" said Jack. He and Annie ran down the embankment toward some woods near the tracks. Then they took off through the brush, weaving around mossy trees and pale spring ferns. They pushed back twigs and vines, trying to get as far away from the train as possible.

"Are we heading in the right direction?" Jack asked, panting.

Annie pulled out the compass and looked at it. "Yes! Southwest!"

"Good! Keep going!" said Jack. They ran until they came to the edge of a road. Up the road, a bridge crossed a wide river. A sign next to the bridge said RIVER ORNE.

"That's the river we want!" cried Annie. *"Cross a river to find a cave!"*

"Cross it!" said Jack. He and Annie hurried to the bridge and raced across the river. On the other side was a small restaurant. A sign on the front said SYLVIE'S BISTRO.

"Stop! Stop!" said Jack, gasping. "Before we go any farther, let's stop there—rest—and make a plan—"

"Great, I'm dying of thirst," said Annie.

They caught their breath. Then they straightened their berets, smiled fake smiles, and walked into the bistro. Inside the crowded dining room, the air smelled of coffee and cigarette smoke. Jack and Annie slipped over to an empty table and sat down.

He reached up and helped Annie drop to the ground, too."

"I'm so sorry," Annie said, leaning toward Jack. "I didn't mean to get you in trouble. I—" Before she could go on, a teenage waitress brought silverware and menus to their table.

"May I help you, sir?" the girl asked Jack.

For a moment, Jack just stared at the dark-haired, rosy-cheeked girl. He was still in a daze both from being arrested and from the explosion.

"Can we have two lemonades, please?" Annie asked.

The waitress nodded and left.

"I'm so sorry!" Annie whispered again to Jack. "When I went down to the cellar to get our stuff, I grabbed a bunch of flyers and put them in your field pack."

"Why?" asked Jack. "Why would you do that?"

"I thought while we were looking for Kathleen, we could do what Tom and Theo did," said Annie. "You know, put up flyers when no one is looking. It seemed like a good—"

"Okay, okay, I get it," said Jack. "But we can't

worry about *their* mission. We have our *own* mission." He reached into his pack and pulled out the flyers. "We have to get rid of these. If we don't—"

"Jack!" Annie said, looking over his shoulder.

Jack turned around. The waitress was standing behind him with their lemonades. When her gaze fell on the flyers in Jack's hand, her eyes widened. Jack clutched the batch of papers to his chest. Without a word, the waitress put down their drinks and hurried to the kitchen at the back of the bistro.

"We have to go," said Jack. "She saw the flyers!" He jammed the papers into his pack.

"Wait," said Annie.

"We can't!" said Jack. "She's gone to tell someone, like her boss. They'll call the police!"

Before Jack and Annie could stand up to leave, the waitress burst out of the kitchen with a tall, stern-looking woman wearing an apron. The woman's heavy shoes clomped on the wooden floor as she headed over to Jack and Annie.

"My mother wants to talk to you," the waitress said.

Oh, no! thought Jack.

The woman pulled up a chair and sat down. She leaned forward. "Tell me, please," she whispered. "How do you know Tom and Theo?"

NINE

CODE BREAKERS

Jack and Annie stared in shock at the woman. Before they could answer, the door to the bistro swung open, and three Nazi soldiers entered. The men ignored everyone as they sat at a corner table not far from Jack and Annie.

The young waitress moved quickly to serve them.

"My name is Sylvie," the girl's mother said softly to Jack and Annie. "I am a friend of the twins. A good friend."

Jack was wary. *Is she really a friend?* he wondered.

Annie did not seem to have the same doubts. "Oh, wow, hi," she said in a low voice. "We know their parents."

"I have never met Tom and Theo's parents," said Sylvie. She glanced at the table in the corner. The Nazis were laughing loudly with her daughter. "In the Resistance, we keep our personal lives secret from each other. That way, other families might avoid punishment if one of us is caught. Do the parents know what happened to their sons?"

"No. Only that they were caught in Paris," said Annie. "They don't know if they're in prison or not."

"Tom and Theo are not in prison. They are safe," Sylvie whispered. "With help from others, they escaped from jail and fled to the south of France. Then they crossed over the Pyrenees mountains into Spain."

"That's great!" whispered Annie.

Jack looked at the Nazis. They were still joking with Sylvie's daughter. Was there any chance Sylvie was working with them? What if this was a trap? Was she making up the story about Tom and Theo?

"Are you sure that's true?" he asked, narrowing his eyes at Sylvie.

"I understand your caution," Sylvie whispered. Then she slowly moved two silver spoons into the shape of a V.

Jack nodded. *Okay,* he thought. He was willing to take the chance that Sylvie was telling the truth.

Sylvie then straightened the spoons. "It is very dangerous for you to carry these flyers," she said under her breath.

"I know. It's my fault," said Annie. "I wanted to help Tom and Theo. We got caught on a train, and Jack was almost arrested. But then the tracks got blown up and we escaped."

Sylvie smiled. "You are brave," she said. "In this time, even children must be brave."

"But helping Tom and Theo isn't really our mission," said Annie. "We're trying to find a friend and help her escape to England."

Jack glanced again at the corner table. The Nazis were studying their menus now.

"Is there any way I can help you?" said Sylvie.

"Yes," said Annie. She slipped Kathleen's rhyme out of her pocket and put it on the table. "Our friend sent us this coded message." Sylvie discreetly looked at the note. "The only lines we don't understand are the last ones."

Jack glanced at the soldiers again. One of them looked up and his gaze rested on Sylvie. "They're watching you," Jack whispered.

Sylvie nodded. Then she laughed. "So you both love apples?" she said.

What is she talking about? Jack wondered. *Is she speaking in code?*

"Yes, we *love* apples," Annie said, smiling.

"What kind of apples do you like best?" Sylvie said.

"Um . . . I like Granny Smith apples," said Annie. "So does Jack."

"Good, good!" said Sylvie. "Well, we have very delicious varieties of apples in this area. They have funny names, such as the Gentle Bishop and Skin of the Dog. But my favorites are the Yellow Knights and the White Calves."

Jack didn't know what to say. He wasn't sure how to play this game.

Annie looked calmly at Jack. *"Yellow knights,"* she said, *"and small, round cows."*

"Oh . . . oh," said Jack. *Apples!* So in her note, Kathleen was secretly writing about *apples*! Not knights! Not cows!

Annie laughed. "And can we find those delicious varieties of apples somewhere near here?" she asked.

"Oh, yes," said Sylvie. "In fact, my bistro is on the Road of Rocks. Down the street is a deserted château with a small orchard. Beautiful Yellow Knights and White Calves grow on trees there. So perhaps that is where you will find what you're looking for." She casually tapped the note. Jack saw that her fingers were pointing to the line *a crack in a rock beneath the boughs.*

"Cool," Jack said. "Thank you."

"You're most welcome," said Sylvie. She stood up and straightened her apron. "Enjoy your day, children. I hope you find the apple of your dreams."

"With your help, I think we will," said Jack. He glanced at the Nazis. The soldier was no longer looking at their table. He was lighting a cigarette and listening to his friends. Jack flashed a quick *V Is for Victory* sign at Sylvie. She smiled, then crossed the dining room back to the kitchen.

"Friend," Annie said to Jack as she put the note back into her pocket.

"Big-time," Jack said. He checked a clock on the wall. "It's almost two. We have six hours left." He took a long sip of lemonade, left some money on the table, and stood up. As he and Annie quietly slipped out of the bistro, he heard the Nazis laughing with each other.

It was still cloudy outside. A damp wind was blowing.

"This is the Road of Rocks," said Annie, looking at a sign. "Now we just need to find a deserted château. What's a château?"

"I think it's like a big, fancy house," said Jack.

"Cool," said Annie. "Let's find it."

"Oh, wait," said Jack. "We have to do something first."

"What?" said Annie.

"Come with me," said Jack. He led the way around the bistro to an open window in the back. Through the window they saw Sylvie in the kitchen. She was stirring a pot on the stove.

Jack looked around to make sure that no one was watching. Then he called in a loud whisper, "Sylvie!"

She looked surprised and came over to the window. "Yes?"

"Could you do us a favor?" said Jack. "Could you send a wireless message to the BBC?"

She nodded.

"Could you have it say . . ." Jack thought for a moment. "Have it say, *Your twin unicorns are free in Spain.*"

Sylvie looked puzzled.

"Tom and Theo," said Jack. "Their parents will

understand what that means when they hear it over their wireless. It will make them very happy."

"Yes," said Sylvie. "I will do that."

"Thanks!" said Jack.

"Good work!" Annie said as she and Jack slipped back around the restaurant.

"Yep," said Jack. "Now, a deserted château with apple trees!"

"Onward!" said Annie.

As they started up the Road of Rocks, Jack and Annie strolled past a couple of houses, a churchyard, and an ancient-looking cemetery. They passed a butcher shop, a bookstore, and a bakery called *La Baguette*.

"I don't get it," said Jack. "Why would Kathleen be hiding in a cave? It seems so safe here. Why doesn't she come out in the open?"

"I was wondering the same thing," said Annie. "And why didn't she just tell Teddy when and where to pick her up and then go there to meet him? You have to be cautious, but you can still travel around. Something's not right."

"Yeah, really," said Jack.

Jack and Annie walked farther up the road and rounded a bend. "Whoa," said Jack. "A deserted château?"

Set against a rocky hillside was a mansion with a sagging roof and broken windows. On its grounds were fallen-down sheds, overgrown gardens, and a scattering of bushes and weeds.

Annie pointed to a cluster of flowering trees in front of the hillside. "Apple orchard," she said. The spring breeze shook their boughs, and white petals floated to the ground like snowflakes.

"Yes!" said Jack. He looked around. No vehicles or pedestrians were close by. "Trespass!"

Jack and Annie walked up the driveway. Their boots crunched over the gravel path as they hurried across the weedy grounds of the château. When they drew close to the hillside, they studied the rocks.

"There," said Annie. She pointed to a crack big enough for a person to slip through.

"Okay," said Jack. "Wait." He reached into his

pack and took out the flashlight Teddy had given them.

"I'll go first," said Annie. She squeezed through the shoulder-wide crack in the rock, and Jack followed her. They stepped into a tunnel, lit only by the shaft of light from the crack.

Jack switched on their flashlight and shined it on the cream-colored stone walls. "This must be one of the limestone tunnels that Suzette and Gaston talked about," he said.

"Listen," said Annie.

Voices were singing deep inside the tunnel—high, sweet voices:

Twinkle, twinkle, little star,
How I wonder what you are.

TEN

HIDEOUT

"What's going on?" Jack whispered.

"Let's find out," said Annie.

Jack turned off the flashlight. The sound of the singing guided them as they tiptoed through the downward-sloping tunnel and into a giant cavern. Across the cavern, candles flickered in a corner. The candlelight shone on a group of small children sitting with a teenage girl. Most of the children were no more than three or four years old. They sat on a pile of blankets, facing the girl as she sang with them:

Twinkle, twinkle, little star,
How I wonder what you are.
Up above the world so high,
Like a diamond in the sky.

The children's bell-like voices were beautiful, Jack thought.

When the blazing sun is gone,
When it nothing shines upon,
Then you show your little light,
Twinkle, twinkle, all the night.

Jack and Annie waited until the children had finished their song. Then Annie called, "Kathleen!"

All the children turned to look. Kathleen let out a cry and hurried across the cavern into Annie's arms. Then she grabbed Jack and hugged him tightly, too.

The enchantress wiped tears from her sea-blue eyes. Her long curly hair was tangled and dirty. She looked tired and thin. "I am so glad to see you!

But what—what are you doing here?" she said. "Where is Teddy?"

"Teddy sent us instead," Jack said, "because he thought we could decode your message."

"Plus he had to save downed airmen in Holland and Belgium," said Annie. "What happened to you? Who are these little kids?"

By now, the children were tugging on Jack's and Annie's overalls, chattering: "Hello!" "Who are you?" "What's your name?" They wore ragged clothes and no shoes, but their small, pale faces were open and trusting.

"Are you taking care of all these kids?" Annie asked Kathleen.

"Yes. I have two wonderful helpers, Sarah and her sister, Sophie," said Kathleen. She pointed to the tallest children in the group. The sisters looked to be about six and seven years old. Their dark eyes shining, they smiled shyly at Jack and Annie.

"These are my friends Jack and Annie," Kathleen said to the children. "They have come a very long way to help us. Jack and Annie, meet Solly, Etty, Daniel, Eli . . ." Kathleen pointed to each tiny child as she said the names. "Pierre, Leo, Marcella and Ella . . ."

Talking over her, the children asked questions all at once: "Who are you?" "Can you stay with us?" "Where do you live?"

"Children, children," Kathleen said in a calm voice. "Hush, please! Go back to your blankets now with Sophie and Sarah, and rest. You can play with Jack and Annie after you wake."

The children did as Kathleen asked. Still chattering, though more softly, they followed the older girls back to their blankets. Sophie and Sarah seemed very grown-up as they tried to settle the younger children down.

"Have you all been living in this cave a long time?" asked Annie.

"This is our hideout during the day," said Kathleen. "After dark, I sneak them into the empty château, and we hide in the attic there. The plumbing still works, and there is fresh well water. I found a supply of candles, thank goodness. Sophie and Sarah are very capable. They watch the others at night while I look for food. I visit gardens and gather old bread from behind the bakery. Before daylight, I lead the children back here. We sing and play games and nap and talk. I don't think they realize that we are in hiding."

"Why do you have to hide them?" asked Jack.

"To keep them safe from the Nazis," said Kathleen. "My assignment with the SOE was to find Sophie and Sarah in a Normandy orphanage and sneak them into England. Their parents had escaped prison and already made their own way to London."

"Why were their mom and dad in prison?" Annie asked.

"Their parents are brilliant scientists. They were both arrested in Paris by the Nazis because they are Jewish," said Kathleen.

"That's crazy," said Annie.

"Yeah," said Jack.

"Yes, it is," said Kathleen. "When I arrived in

Normandy, I found that the orphanage had been abandoned, but there were still children there. Sophie and Sarah were taking care of them as best they could. Because all the children were Jewish, I needed to hide them."

"Oh, man," said Jack. He couldn't understand why the Nazis hated Jewish people so much. He'd read about it and seen movies about it, but he'd never understood it.

"There are too many for me to get them all to safety," said Kathleen. "That is why I sent word to Teddy that I needed magic. I wanted something to make us invisible or something to help us fly. If only I could turn them into little birds, I thought, they could fly across the channel and then become themselves again."

"Right," said Annie, smiling, "like when you once turned us into seals off the coast of Ireland?"

"Exactly like that," said Kathleen.

"Well, why do you need magic from Teddy?" asked Jack. "What happened to your own magic powers?"

"I do not know." Kathleen shook her head. "I—I seem to have lost part of myself here. I fear that sadness and worry have drained me of my ability to perform magic. . . . Perhaps being terrified for the children . . ." She shook her head again. "But you have brought help, yes? The wand?"

Jack took a deep breath. "Actually, no, we didn't," he answered. "No magic. Only ourselves."

Kathleen looked confused. "But in my message—"

"I know," said Annie. "Teddy meant to give us the Wand of Dianthus, but he forgot. He was flying the plane and helping us learn how to parachute and somehow he forgot, and *we* forgot, too."

"I remembered just as we were about to jump out of the plane," said Jack. "But then it was too late."

"He forgot? I cannot believe it. How could he?" Kathleen's voice trembled. "Oh, that is terrible. . . . Only magic can help these children escape harm. We cannot leave France now. We are trapped."

"You *have* to leave," said Jack. "We *all* have to leave France by nightfall. A giant military invasion is starting tomorrow. It's called the D-Day invasion. We heard that bombs will be dropped over this whole area."

Kathleen shook her head. "No . . . I—I don't know how we can leave. . . . No, it is not possible," she stammered.

Jack couldn't believe how much Kathleen had changed, from a joyful, confident person to someone much more worried and fragile. He found his own confidence starting to fail. "I don't know what to do," he said, looking at Annie.

"Well," said Annie, "*I* know what to do. We're going to get all these kids and ourselves out of France by nightfall. We have skills."

"What skills?" said Jack.

"Um . . . skills, you know, you said so yourself. Remember in the ditch?" said Annie.

Jack couldn't think of a single skill that would help their situation.

"Don't worry," Annie said. "We have courage. We have hope. And we have each other. So let's make a plan."

Jack just stared at her.

Annie went on. "First of all," she said, "with all these kids, we won't be able to fit into Teddy's little plane." She turned to Kathleen. "We already sent a message to Teddy telling him to pick us up at nightfall at the same spot where he dropped us off. So now we just need to send a message telling him to bring a bigger plane."

"Sylvie at the bistro can do that," said Jack. Annie's confidence was lifting his spirits.

"Good idea," said Annie. "Next we have to figure out how to get from here back to the drop zone."

"That's the hard part," said Jack. "We need . . . a truck or something . . . like the milk truck that took us to Caen. . . ."

"Right," said Annie. "So the kids can hide in the back."

Kathleen's face lit up. "Oh! Every night I go to the bakery up the street after it closes," she said. "There is always a delivery truck parked in the driveway. It is never locked. I know this because

I gather scraps of stale bread from the back."

"Okay," said Jack. "But there's only one problem: if we borrow that truck, who's going to drive it?"

"*You,* silly!" said Annie.

"*Me?*" said Jack.

"Yes, you!" Annie turned to Kathleen. "Jack's not old enough to have a license, but he learned how to drive an old truck on our great-grandfather's farm. He's only allowed to drive around the pastures, but he's a good driver! That's one of his skills!"

"No!" said Jack.

"Yes!" said Annie. "So all we have to do is gather the kids, use the truck to get them to the drop zone, wait for Teddy to show up with a bigger plane, get everybody on board, and we're all out of here by nightfall."

"Fantastic!" said Kathleen. "We have a plan!"

ELEVEN

The Plan

Kathleen's sea-blue eyes were sparkling. "I will go tell Sophie and Sarah to get the children ready!" She hurried across the cavern.

Jack whirled around to Annie. "No, no, no!" he whispered. "This is not a good plan."

"It is! You drove Great-Granddad's truck perfectly just a few weeks ago!" said Annie. "I was there! I wanted to drive it, too, but I couldn't reach the pedals."

"But that—" said Jack.

"You didn't even need a key with that old

truck," said Annie. "Remember? You just turned the starter switch. You learned how to use the clutch and the gearshift. You drove us around the field for hours—around and around and around. You always say you can't wait to drive that truck again!"

"But this is so different!" said Jack.

"It's not *that* different," Annie said.

"Are you crazy? It's totally different!" said Jack. "Stealing a truck, loading it with tiny kids, and driving through a foreign country to try to escape Nazis in World War Two is *totally* different from driving in a circle in our great-grandfather's pasture."

"Okay. It's different," said Annie.

"Thank you!" said Jack.

"It's different because there are lives at stake here," said Annie. "And that's why *you have to do it.*"

Before Jack could say anything, Kathleen came rushing back. She was holding a candle and a folded map. "What was the location of your drop zone?" she asked.

"It's a field in Biéville, next to a church," said Annie. "Six miles northwest of Caen."

"Good," said Kathleen. "I have the Normandy map the SOE gave me. It will help us. Let's go get the truck." By the light of her candle, she led the way out of the cavern and through the limestone tunnel.

Jack's heart was racing. Annie was right. Lives were at stake. But he was already sweating, and they hadn't even started the plan yet! How would he feel when he was trying to sneak a truckload of Jewish orphans past Nazi soldiers?

Jack and Annie followed Kathleen through the tunnel to the crack in the rock. Then they walked into the gray light of late afternoon. The wind blew softly over the grounds of the château as they headed down the driveway.

"Let's refine our plan," said Kathleen. She sounded more like her old self. "Sophie and Sarah will get the children ready. Annie will go to Sylvie at the bistro and ask her to send a new message to Teddy. Jack and I will pick up the bakery truck.

Then we will all meet back here, load up the children, and head for the drop zone."

"Got it," said Annie.

Jack nodded. He was relieved that Kathleen seemed so much stronger. He hoped it meant her magic skills would soon return. Right now he thought they *really* needed a little magic.

When they came to the road, Kathleen turned to Annie. "You should go ahead of us to Sylvie," she said, "so we will not look as if we are traveling in a group. The Nazis do not like groups."

"Okay, meet you guys back here," said Annie. "Good luck!" She started walking up the Road of Rocks toward Sylvie's Bistro.

Jack took a deep breath as he and Kathleen stood together waiting for Annie to get a good distance away. He always felt shy when he was alone with the beautiful enchantress.

"Jack, these have been the two worst weeks of my life," Kathleen said, breaking the silence. "I knew it was possible I could be responsible for the loss of ten children. I felt helpless and sad and angry all at once. I have never felt that way before."

"You're not helpless, Kathleen," said Jack. "You're strong and—and you're good. That's why you were sad and angry."

"Thank you, Jack," she said. "I am very, very relieved you and Annie came to help."

"We haven't really done anything yet," Jack said.

"But you will," she said. "I admire you very much." She looked up the Road of Rocks. "Annie is far enough ahead, I think. We can go now."

Jack straightened his shoulders as he and Kathleen walked together up the road. He was ready to drive the truck. In fact, he was ready to do anything to be worthy of Kathleen's admiration.

The bakery was closed when they got there. No one was on the sidewalk.

"The delivery truck should be in back," said Kathleen. "Come with me." She and Jack slipped behind the building.

An old-fashioned cream-colored truck was parked behind the bakery. The cab of the truck looked just like the cab of Jack's great-grandfather's truck. The back was different, though. His great-grandfather's truck was a pickup, but the back of this truck was box-shaped like a van. The words LA BAGUETTE were painted on the side.

Jack looked at the bakery truck. He took a deep breath. "Okay, this should work," he said, trying to sound calm. "Let's see how she looks inside." He pulled on the handle of the cab, and the door swung open.

Jack stuck his head inside and saw that the truck had a keyless starter switch, just like his great-grandfather's truck. He turned back to Kathleen. "We're in business," he said.

"Wonderful!" Kathleen said. "Do you have a piece of paper so I can leave a note for the baker?"

Jack reached into his pack and gave Kathleen his notebook and a pencil. She wrote on a blank page:

> Thank you for letting us borrow your truck. It is waiting for you near the church in Biéville.

She tore the paper out of Jack's notebook, folded it, and slid it under the back door of the bakery. Then they both climbed into the front seat. "Good to go?" Jack asked.

"Yes!" she said, smiling. "Good to go."

Jack looked at the floor and found the clutch pedal on the left, the brake in the middle, and the gas pedal on the right, just like in his great-grandfather's truck. He put his hand on the gearshift next to his seat. Everything felt familiar. "Okey-dokey," he said. "Let's get this show on the road."

Jack pressed the brake with his right foot and then pushed the clutch pedal down with his left. He moved the gearshift into neutral. Then he turned the starter switch, and the engine rumbled to life.

Jack shifted into first gear. He moved his right foot off the brake and pressed the gas pedal. The truck engine roared. Jack took his foot off the clutch. The truck jerked forward and the engine stopped dead.

"No problem, no problem," said Jack. "It'll just

take me a minute to get the hang of it again."

Jack repeated everything he had done: brake, clutch, gearshift into neutral, starter, gearshift into first. This time, he operated the clutch and gas pedals perfectly, and the bakery truck moved smoothly onto the Road of Rocks.

"Brilliant!" said Kathleen. "We are on our way!"

As Jack headed up the street, he kept all his attention on his driving, not daring to think of their plan. Instead, he imagined he was just driving around his great-grandfather's pasture.

When the truck came to the old château, Annie was heading into the driveway. Seeing Jack behind the wheel, she raised her arms skyward and jumped up and down as if he'd just crossed a finish line.

Jack and Kathleen laughed as Annie ran alongside the truck, waving her arms. Jack brought the bakery truck to a stop near the hillside. Then he and Kathleen climbed out.

"You did it! You did it!" Annie said to Jack.

He shrugged as if it was no big deal.

"Wait here. I will get the children," said Kathleen. "Sophie and Sarah should have them ready by now." She dashed to the rocks.

"Was it hard to drive?" Annie asked Jack.

"Not once I got it going," he said. "It all kind of came back to me. Did you give the message to Sylvie?"

"Yes! I snuck around the back of the bistro and tapped on the window again," said Annie. "I asked her to send another message, one that said, 'Unicorn has ten colts. Need bigger bird.'"

"Good work," said Jack.

"Here they come," said Annie.

Kathleen, Sophie, and Sarah led the small children out of the tunnel. Excited to go for a ride, the little kids raced across the grass to the bakery truck. Jack got out and swung open the rear door. Then he, Annie, and Kathleen lifted each child into the back.

"Is everyone here?" called Kathleen. She called out all their names to make sure: "Ella? Eli? Leo? Daniel? . . ."

La Baguette
272 M141

"Seeing Jack behind the wheel, she raised her arms skyward and jumped up and down as if he'd just crossed a finish line."

As each high voice rang out "Yes!" Jack climbed into the driver's seat. Soon Kathleen and Annie joined him. Jack could hear the children chattering behind the partition that separated the cab from the back.

"They are so excited," said Kathleen.

"It smells like bread back there," said Annie. "The children found lots of old crusts to eat."

"Really?" said Jack. He could hear their voices saying: "This is good!" "I love it!" "It's hard to chew." "Yes, but it's very good!"

Jack's throat tightened. He wanted only one thing in the world right now—to help these little kids escape from France.

TWELVE

Checkpoint

Kathleen opened the map of the Caen area and showed it to Annie.

"Mondeville . . . ," Annie said, pointing. "And Biéville. It looks like we have about seven miles to go."

"All set?" said Jack. He took a breath. He started the truck, shifted into gear, then drove down the driveway toward the road.

"Turn right," said Kathleen, studying the map.

Jack turned right. He drove faster and shifted gears as they moved up the quiet Road of Rocks.

"Left onto Calmette Street," said Kathleen, "then right onto Clopee."

Jack followed her directions.

"Right onto Cabourg," said Annie, "then a quick left."

Jack turned onto Cabourg, then made a quick left—and landed in the middle of a traffic jam!

"Oh, no," Kathleen said quietly.

Up the road, Nazi soldiers were stopping traffic. Two of the Nazis held up spotlights as vehicles crawled toward them.

"What's going on?" asked Annie.

"It's a checkpoint," said Kathleen.

Jack stopped breathing. "What does that mean?" he asked.

"It means officials randomly stop vehicles and check identities," said Kathleen.

The soldiers waved one car through, but they stopped the next. Traffic came to a halt as a Nazi official shined a flashlight into the car that had stopped.

"Oh, man," said Jack. When he saw another

Nazi inspect the car's trunk, he started to panic. He was terrified that the soldiers would stop them, too, and look in the back of the bakery truck.

"Tell the kids to be quiet," Jack said.

Kathleen tapped on the partition. "Quiet, please, children! You must be very quiet now! Not one word!"

The children were silent. Jack gripped the steering wheel to try to stop his hands from shaking.

"Jack, you have to look calm," said Kathleen. "You must look as if you drive this truck every day to deliver bread."

"Yeah, like it's no big deal," said Annie.

"I—I don't think I can—" Jack said in a strangled voice.

"You have to!" said Annie.

"Wait . . . wait a moment!" said Kathleen. She closed her eyes and opened them. "Oh, my!"

"What is it?" asked Jack.

"I just recalled a spell that will keep us safe!" she said.

"Really?" said Jack.

"Yes. Since being with you and Annie, I have grown more hopeful. I think that feeling of hope is bringing back some of my magic!" said Kathleen.

"That's wonderful!" said Annie. "What's the spell you remember?"

"It is a spell to make us invisible," said Kathleen.

"Really?" said Jack.

"Yes, drive on, Jack," said Kathleen. The cars had started moving again. "Do not look to either side—stare straight ahead."

As Jack shifted from neutral into first gear and then second, Kathleen closed her eyes and whispered a rhyme:

Powers of goodness, powers of light,
Shield us now from powers of sight.

When Kathleen started to repeat the rhyme, Annie closed her eyes and joined in:

Powers of goodness, powers of light,
Shield us now from powers of sight.

Holding his breath and staring straight ahead, Jack drove toward the checkpoint.

Powers of goodness, powers of light,
Shield us now from powers of sight.

Kathleen opened her eyes and looked around. "It worked," she whispered. "We are invisible."

"We are?" said Jack. "How do you know?"

"The Nazis are completely ignoring us," said Kathleen. "They see nothing but empty space between the car in front of us and the car behind us. When it is our turn to pass the checkpoint, be calm and drive straight through."

Jack relaxed a little as he imagined being invisible. Kathleen whispered the magic spell again:

Powers of goodness, powers of light,
Shield us now from powers of sight.

The soldiers waved at the driver of the green

car ahead of the bakery truck, giving permission for it to move on.

"Good," said Kathleen. "Now just follow closely behind that car and we will be fine."

Jack fixed his eyes on the back of the green car. Following it, he drove steadily and calmly past the checkpoint. When he glanced in the rearview mirror, he saw that the soldiers were paying no attention at all to the bakery truck. He had no doubt now that Kathleen's magic was working. They were definitely invisible.

"Drive on, Jack," said Kathleen.

Jack drove on. When he looked in his rearview mirror again, he saw the soldiers stopping the car behind them.

"We made it!" said Annie.

"Yes," said Kathleen, looking at the map. "Turn left here, Jack. Then an immediate right and follow the sign to St. Clair."

Jack did as Kathleen said. He turned left, then right, and pressed harder on the gas pedal. The road ahead was empty. He drove faster and faster, shifting into third gear. In the fading light of dusk, the truck glided along the smooth road.

"Yay," said Annie. "I think we'll make it by nightfall!"

Jack said nothing. He was afraid to break the spell of invisibility.

"When you see a sign for Biéville, turn right," said Kathleen.

Jack nodded and kept driving.

"Biéville!" said Annie.

Jack turned right.

"Church!" said Annie.

The white steeple of the church was rising into the darkening sky. Next to the church was the drop zone, the empty field where they had landed with their parachutes.

"That's where Teddy will pick us up," said Annie.

"Good. Drive to the back of the church," said Kathleen, "so the truck cannot be seen."

How can the truck be seen from anywhere? Jack wondered. *Has Kathleen undone her spell?*

He pulled off the road and bumped over the grass to the back of the church. When he brought the truck to a stop and switched off the engine, Kathleen and Annie clapped.

"We're here! We made it!" said Annie.

"You were brilliant, Jack!" said Kathleen.

"Oh, no, you get the credit," he said. "I could never have done it without your magic."

"Yes, you could have," said Kathleen. "In fact, you *did.*"

"What?" said Jack.

"Jack, I fear I did not tell you the truth," said Kathleen. "I still do not have magic powers. I did not make us invisible with a spell."

"You didn't?" said Annie.

"No," said Kathleen. "I knew that as long as Jack felt confident, an ordinary bakery truck would not draw the attention of the Nazis. I felt sure we could slip safely by."

"Oh, brother," said Jack. He took a deep breath. He didn't know whether to be angry with

Kathleen or amazed at himself. In his confusion, he just laughed. Annie and Kathleen joined in. *Well, at least the scariest part of the journey is over,* Jack thought.

Kathleen, Jack, and Annie climbed out of the cab. The countryside was quiet. No vehicles were in sight, and no dogs were barking. The moon was on the horizon.

"I hope Teddy received the messages from Gaston and Sylvie," said Jack, "or else we'll all be stranded here during the D-Day invasion."

"Tell me, what *is* the D-Day invasion?" asked Kathleen.

"Sometime after midnight, more than a hundred thousand Allied soldiers will invade by sea and air to drive the Nazis out of France," said Jack. "It will be the beginning of the end of World War Two."

"That is good. Very good," breathed Kathleen. "All the world is living a great nightmare now. When it wakes, everyone will wonder how this could have happened, and I fear no one will know the answer." She shook her head. "Well, what should we do now?"

"I think maybe we should do a better job of hiding the truck," said Jack, looking around.

"You and I can move it down the road," said Annie.

"While you do that, I will hide the children in the church," said Kathleen.

"Good plan," said Jack. "We'll help you get them inside."

Kathleen, Jack, and Annie walked to the rear of the truck. When Kathleen opened the door, they found the children sprawled all over the back, fast asleep. Even Sophie and Sarah had closed their eyes. "Wake up, birdies," Kathleen sang softly. "Wake up."

Her sweet voice roused the children from sleep. As they began to stir, some reached out and put their arms around Jack, Annie, and Kathleen. Jack gently lifted Leo and Eli out of the back of the truck. Then he clutched their hands and walked with them across the grass. "Let's go inside this nice building," he said. "It's peaceful in there."

"Is this our new house?" Leo asked, rubbing his eyes.

"Can you live here with us?" said Eli.

Jack led his two sleepy three-year-olds into the church, while Annie, Kathleen, Sophie, and Sarah shepherded the others after him.

Inside the dark front entrance, the air smelled of old wood and incense. The last light of day shone through stained-glass windows. After Jack, Annie, and Kathleen got everyone settled in the front pew, Kathleen started to lead the children in song.

"Let's move the truck now," Jack said to Annie. She nodded. As they slipped down the aisle and out of the church, they heard:

Are you sleeping, are you sleeping,
Brother John, Brother John?
Morning bells are ringing,
Morning bells are ringing,
Ding dong ding, ding dong ding.

THIRTEEN

Searchlights

Night was falling fast as Jack and Annie climbed back into the bakery truck.

"We shouldn't drive far," said Jack. "Kathleen left a note for the baker, telling him to look for his truck near the church in Biéville. I hope he's still alive tomorrow and comes to get it."

"You hope he's still alive tomorrow?" said Annie. "That sounds terrible."

"I know," said Jack. "War is terrible." He started the truck, and they bumped back over the grass to the road. Jack drove about a hundred yards, then pulled off the road and parked the bakery truck beside a clump of trees. "I think this should do it," he said.

Annie hopped out of the truck. Jack switched off the motor and rolled up his window. Then he climbed out, too. "Let's hurry—"

"Look, Jack." Annie sounded scared. "Look up."

Jack looked up. Two giant beams of light were sweeping across the sky, crisscrossing each other.

"What's going on?" asked Annie.

"Those lights must be looking for planes to shoot down," said Jack.

"Oh, no!" said Annie. "What if they spot Teddy's plane?"

Jack didn't answer right away. *Maybe the worst isn't over yet,* he thought. "Let's hurry back and tell Kathleen," he said.

Jack and Annie ran up the road to the church. Inside, they found Kathleen still singing with the children.

Row, row, row your boat
Gently down the stream.
Merrily, merrily, merrily, merrily,
Life is but a dream.

Our plan isn't going to work, Jack thought. He felt sure that the Nazis would spot Teddy's plane and shoot it down before he could land.

"Kathleen!" Annie called.

Kathleen told the children to keep singing, and she hurried over to Jack and Annie. "What's wrong?" she asked.

"The Nazis are using searchlights to spot planes," said Jack. "They're sure to see Teddy."

"Show me," said Kathleen.

Jack and Annie led Kathleen outside. The lights were still sweeping across the night sky.

"See?" said Jack, pointing up at the moving beams of light. "How can Teddy possibly—"

Annie gasped. "Look!" she said. "Look at the field!"

Below the dazzling searchlights, a silver plane sat in the dark field. The gleaming plane was much bigger than a spy taxi. It had a snub-nosed cockpit, a long row of windows, and four huge propellers—two on each wing.

"Where did that come from?" said Kathleen.

"I don't know," said Jack, stunned. "I didn't see it when we moved the truck or came back to the church. I didn't hear it fly overhead or land or anything!"

The rear door of the plane swung open. Silhouetted in the doorway was a person in a flight suit and helmet.

"Teddy!" said Annie.

"Oh!" cried Kathleen. She dashed across the dark field. Jack and Annie ran after her.

When Kathleen reached Teddy, she threw her arms around him. Jack and Annie piled on, and they all hugged him at the same time. Everyone was laughing.

"I'm so glad you got our messages!" said Annie.

"So am I!" said Teddy.

"Do you know that D-Day is tomorrow?" asked Jack.

"Yes, I found out today," said Teddy. "With all the preparations for the invasion, I had trouble finding a big enough plane to come for you. But finally I was able to call upon a friend to help me."

"Great!" said Annie.

"How did the plane land without the search-lights spotting it?" asked Jack. "And why didn't it make any noise?"

"I will explain later," said Teddy. "We must act quickly. You have others with you, no?"

"Oh, yes, lots of others!" said Annie.

"This way!" said Kathleen. She grabbed Teddy's hand and pulled him toward the church.

"Kathleen rescued ten little kids from an abandoned orphanage," Annie said.

"That's why she couldn't get out of France," said Jack.

"Oh, no!" Teddy whirled around to Kathleen. "I should have come myself to save you!"

"Do not feel bad," said Kathleen. "Jack and Annie have given me miraculous help, and all without magic. I have lost my powers, Teddy."

"I gathered that from your message," said Teddy. "That is why I sent you the wand and—" He stopped and smacked his forehead. "Oh, no! I forgot, didn't I?"

"You did," said Jack. "But it's not all your fault. Annie and I forgot, too, until just before I jumped. And then it was too late."

"I am so sorry!" said Teddy.

"It's okay," said Annie. "You had a lot on your mind."

"No, it is unforgivable!" said Teddy.

"Seriously, it's okay," said Jack. "We managed."

By then they had arrived at the door of the church. "Get ready to be mobbed by little kids," Annie said to Teddy.

Kathleen led the way inside. "Sarah! Sophie! We are leaving!"

Led by the two sisters, all the children clambered toward the door of the church. They gathered around Teddy, asking questions.

"Hush, children, hush now," said Kathleen. "Everyone grab someone's hand. Etty, take Sophie's hand. Daniel, take Sarah's hand. Leo and Eli, Jack's hands. Marcella and Ella, Annie's hands. Pierre and Solly, Teddy's hands. Come along now. Follow me! We are about to go on a great adventure!"

With little hands tucked into bigger hands, everyone followed Kathleen out of the church into the field.

"Oh, look!" said Leo.

"Pretty plane!" said Eli.

"Yes," said Jack, walking with the two boys. "Let's run! We're going to fly through the air on the silver bird!" Gripping their hands, he ran with little steps so the kids could keep up.

When they reached the plane, Teddy took charge. "Big kids help small kids up the stepladder," he said.

Kathleen lifted two preschoolers up to the rear door. Annie climbed up with two more. Sophie and

Sarah each helped a smaller child. Jack held on to Leo and Eli and led them up the steps.

Boarding last, Teddy squeezed into the passenger cabin with Pierre and Solly. Then he closed the heavy door and latched it. "Sit down. Relax, everyone!" he said. "We don't have far to go!"

The little kids laughed and squealed as they scrambled into seats. Some of them jumped into Kathleen's and Annie's laps. Others climbed onto Teddy, all chirping at once.

"Wait a minute," said Jack. "Teddy, aren't you going up to the cockpit to fly the plane?"

"No. As I said, I called on a friend to help me," said Teddy. "He is the pilot."

"Oh," said Jack. "But how did he land without our hearing him? And how did he get past the searchlights?"

"Explanations later," said Teddy. "I think we are about to take off." He said something else, but his voice was drowned out by kids still asking questions: "Where are we going?" "Who are you?" "Is Kathleen your sister?"

As Kathleen and Teddy laughed and tried to answer the children, Jack thought that Kathleen was completely her old self again. Her eyes were bright; her laughter was lighthearted.

Jack looked out the window. The searchlights were still combing the dark for incoming planes. *So how did the SOE pilot land the plane?* he wondered. *And how will he take off without being seen?*

The large silver plane started moving. It moved across the grass with no bumping and no engine sounds—no whirring, roaring, or rumbling.

This is so weird, thought Jack. *Did they make super-silent spy planes in World War Two?* He would have to look it up, he thought. Before he knew it, the plane had lifted off the ground and was gliding through the night with no vibration, rocking, or shaking.

"Can we open a window?" asked Annie.

"No, silly, not on a plane," said Jack.

"Oh, but on *this* plane we can open windows," said Teddy. He leaned over, undid a latch, and pushed open the glass.

As cool air rushed inside the cabin, Annie grabbed Jack's field pack. Without a word, she pulled out the flyers made by the resistance fighters, Tom and Theo. She showed the printed message to Teddy and Kathleen.

They both grinned and nodded.

Then, one at a time, Annie released the flyers out the open window: one, two, three, four, five . . . ten sheets of paper flapped into the moonlit night.

"That's all," said Annie. "I wish I had more."

Kathleen looked at Annie for a moment. Then she smiled and rose from her seat. She pointed her finger at the flyers fluttering toward the earth below. She whispered some words:

Ain solas keng dural ay du!
Annie's wish shall now come true!

Through the window, Jack saw the flyers begin to multiply . . . from ten to a hundred . . . from a hundred to a thousand . . . from a thousand to ten thousand!

"Jack saw the flyers begin to multiply . . ."

HOPE AND COURAGE! FREEDOM SOON!
HOPE AND COURAGE!

Everyone gasped and clapped.

Kathleen's magic was working again! Now that she was with Teddy, now that she was flying home to England, now that she was saving the children, her joy—her magic—had returned!

As the plane crossed the English Channel, the flyers kept multiplying across the sea. Like white petals falling from apple trees, the sheets of paper tumbled and swirled through the air. Tom and Theo's message filled the night sky, gleaming with their bright words:

HOPE AND COURAGE!
FREEDOM SOON!

FOURTEEN

THE PILOT

Soon after the silver plane crossed the English Channel, it landed silently in the field near Glastonbury Tor. Teddy opened the rear door and lowered the stepladder. "Everyone out!" he said.

Once again, the big kids helped the little kids. Everyone climbed down the ladder and stepped onto the dark, dewy grass. The moon was high in the sky now. Jack could hardly believe that he and Annie had only been away from England—and home—for twenty-four hours.

"The SOE has arranged to take everyone to

London," Teddy said to Kathleen. "Motorcars are waiting in the parking lot. This way—"

As Teddy led the group toward the parking lot, Annie carried Daniel and Etty, and Jack carried Leo and Eli.

"Where are we going?" Eli asked him.

"To a safe city," answered Jack. "You'll live in a nice house soon, I promise."

The small boy kissed Jack on the cheek. Then Leo kissed Jack, too. Jack just laughed. "You guys are funny," he said.

"Is Jack your brother?" Etty asked Annie.

"Yes," said Annie. "He's my brother."

"Is he the best brother in the world?" asked the tiny girl.

"Yes, he is," said Annie.

"Are you and Annie coming with us?" Eli asked Jack.

"No, we have to go back to America now," said Jack.

"How will you get there?" asked Leo.

"In a magic tree house," said Jack.

"Can we play in your tree house someday?" asked Leo.

"Absolutely," said Jack. "When you come to America, you can do anything you want."

Three big black cars were waiting in the parking lot beside the airfield. Teddy got four of the children settled in the first car, and Jack and Annie tucked their four into the second car. "See ya, guys," Jack said. "Be good."

Jack closed the door and stood in the dark with Annie and Teddy, as Kathleen guided Sophie and Sarah to the third car in the lot. Before they reached it, the doors opened, and a man and woman climbed out. They were tall and well-dressed.

When the man and woman saw Sophie and Sarah, they both burst into sobs. The man knelt and held out his arms. "My babies . . . ," he said, grabbing Sophie and Sarah and pulling them close. Sophie and Sarah started crying, too. "Papa, Mama! Papa, Mama!"

For a long time, Sophie, Sarah, and their parents all held each other and cried. They were still holding on to each other as they stumbled back to their car and climbed into the backseat together.

Jack felt tears on his cheeks. Kathleen and Annie were sniffling. Teddy cleared his throat and clapped his hands together. "Victory!" he said.

"Victory," said Jack, smiling. Then he held up two fingers.

"What about Eli and Eddie and Leo and all the other kids?" Annie asked Kathleen. "What will happen to them?"

"The SOE will locate relatives and friends to care for them," said Kathleen. "I will go to London and protect them until they are all safely placed in happy homes."

"Thank you for saving them," said Annie.

"Thank *you*, Annie," said Kathleen, "for remaining hopeful and helping make a plan when we were almost ready to give up."

"No problem," said Annie.

"Together, you and Jack saved their lives and mine," said Kathleen. "You are my heroes."

Jack shrugged. "I'm not a hero," he said.

Kathleen took Jack's hand. She looked into his eyes. "You *are* a hero, Jack. Believe me. And you are a wonderful truck driver, too."

Jack laughed.

Kathleen smiled her radiant smile. "Well, until we meet again, farewell," she said. "Teddy? Are you coming?"

"Yes! I will join you for the ride to London," Teddy said. "Wait for me."

"Good." Kathleen blew Jack and Annie a kiss. Then she climbed into the first car.

Teddy turned to them. "If you have a minute before you leave, the pilot of the plane would like to see you," he said.

"Great!" said Jack. He had lots of questions for that SOE pilot—like what kind of plane was he flying?

Teddy, Jack, and Annie hurried away from the parking lot across the grounds of the ancient abbey. In the moonlight, Jack looked back at the landing field. The silver plane wasn't there.

"Where did it go?" he asked, hurrying alongside Teddy. "The plane?"

"Ah, yes. The plane is gone, but the pilot remains behind," Teddy said mysteriously. "Come with me."

Through the misty air, they passed the glistening pond and the sheep asleep in the grass. Just beyond a hedgerow were the ruins of pillars and archways.

"There, on that bench," said Teddy.

Jack could barely make out a person sitting on a stone bench. The person's back was to them, and he was wearing a dark cloak.

"Ohhh," Annie said with a grin. "Got it."

"Got what?" said Jack.

"Got the *whole* thing," said Annie. "I just figured it out!" She hurried to the bench and sat next to the man in the cloak. The next moment, they were talking softly together. The man had a deep voice.

"*Whoa,*" said Jack. Suddenly he got it, too.

He walked over and sat down next to Annie and the man. "Hi, Merlin," Jack said as casually as he could.

"Good evening, Jack," Merlin said. The magician was wearing a black cloak with the cowl over his head. His long white beard shone in the moonlight.

"So Teddy sent for you?" Jack asked.

"Yes," said Merlin.

"And you knew how to find and fly a special military plane?" said Jack.

"No," said the magician of Camelot. "I knew how to *conjure* a special plane to suit your needs, one that could carry fourteen passengers and take off and land without being seen or heard."

"Cool," Jack murmured, still trying to sound cool.

"I know this was an especially difficult mission for you," said Merlin. "You experienced firsthand what it means to live in constant terror."

"Yes," said Jack.

"You know what it feels like to be afraid to

speak or move about freely," said Merlin.

"We do," said Annie.

"You have seen cruel people hunt down the innocent—even children," said Merlin.

Jack and Annie nodded.

"But you overcame your fears in order to accomplish your mission," said Merlin. "Teddy found two excellent recruits in the fight for freedom. There is no way I can adequately thank you. But allow me to try: Thank you. Both of you. And I hope to see you again soon."

"You too," said Annie.

"Anytime," said Jack.

Merlin stood up from the bench. "Well, goodbye," he said. "Have a safe trip home."

"Bye," said Annie.

Jack and Annie watched the master magician walk off into the night and disappear like smoke among the ruins.

"Wow," Annie breathed.

"Wow, indeed," said Teddy, stepping from the shadows. "Now are you ready to go home?"

Jack and Annie stood up from the bench and followed Teddy to the tree house.

Teddy's large duffel bag sat at the base of the tree. Teddy reached in and pulled out their sneakers and Jack's pack. "You can have your things back now," he said.

"Thanks," said Jack. "And you can have your things back, too."

Jack and Annie pulled off their farm boots, overalls, and shirts. Jack shivered in his shorts and T-shirt as he and Annie changed into their sneakers and tied the laces. Then Jack took his pencil and notebook out of the field pack and handed the pack to Teddy. "Thanks for lending this to us," he said.

"You are welcome," said Teddy. "I will have to make up a good story for Winston about how I got all of you out of France. But now I had better catch my ride to London. Until next time—cheerio, chaps."

"Cheerio, chap," Jack and Annie said together.

"Onward!" said Teddy. Then he slung his

duffel bag over his shoulder and headed toward the parking lot.

Jack and Annie watched Teddy march briskly toward the hedgerow. Just before he rounded the corner, he turned and gave them a salute. Then he was gone.

Jack and Annie climbed the rope ladder into the tree house. Annie grabbed the Pennsylvania book. "Ready?" she said.

"Wait." Jack heard the steady hum of planes overhead. He and Annie looked up at the night sky and saw distant lights.

"I wonder if those are D-Day planes," Annie said.

"Yeah, I wonder if they're heading to Normandy," said Jack.

The planes kept moving through the night sky—more planes and more and more.

"It's time for us to go home," said Annie.

"Definitely," said Jack.

Annie pointed to a photo of the Frog Creek

woods. "I wish we could go there," she said.

The wind started to blow.

The tree house started to spin.

It spun faster and faster.

Then everything was still.

Absolutely still.

❦ ❦ ❦

Frog Creek was warm in the summer sunset. Jack breathed in the smell of dry wood and green leaves. He felt as if he had never smelled anything so good and so safe.

"Nice," said Annie.

Jack just nodded. His heart was heavy, too heavy to talk about all they'd seen and done. He picked up his backpack and climbed down the rope ladder. Annie followed. In silence, they started through the late-summer woods, crossing in and out of dark shadows.

"War really is a terrible thing," Annie said finally.

Jack nodded.

"I don't understand it!" said Annie. "Why would *anyone* want to hurt people like Sophie and Sarah and their parents? Or Tom and Theo? Or the old man at the train station?"

"I don't know," said Jack.

"And how could anyone want to hurt those little kids?" said Annie. "What if the Nazis had caught Leo and Eli and all the others?"

Jack shuddered. It was unbearable to think about.

"Germany, England, France, Italy, and the United States—they all work together now for peace in the world, right?" said Annie.

"Right," said Jack. "They're all good friends."

"And the United States and Japan also fought each other in World War Two," said Annie. "But now they're good friends?"

"Right," said Jack.

"Cool," said Annie. "Let's think about that instead, and let's think about Gaston, Suzette, Sylvie, Tom, Theo, and the driver of the milk truck, all trying to do the right thing. During war, I think lots of people try to do the right thing. Don't you?"

"Yes," said Jack.

Jack and Annie left the shadowy woods and crossed their street to the bright, sunshiny sidewalk. The warmth and beauty of the light lifted Jack's spirits.

"I love our lives," Annie said with a sigh.

"Yeah, me too," said Jack. "Especially our freedom."

"Like the freedom to ride our bikes to the lake and the library," said Annie. "The freedom to watch movies and eat popcorn and play Scrabble with Mom and Dad and cook outside on the grill and visit our grandparents . . . and our great-grandparents."

"Yeah, a million things like that," said Jack. Right now, he had a whole new appreciation for the familiar, ordinary things in life.

Jack and Annie turned into their yard and climbed the steps to the front porch. Before Jack opened the screen door, he looked at Annie. "Hey, did you think the airplane pilot would turn out to be Merlin?" he asked.

"No way. I definitely did *not* see that coming," said Annie. "Did you?"

"Not in a million years," Jack said with a grin. Then he headed inside their house.

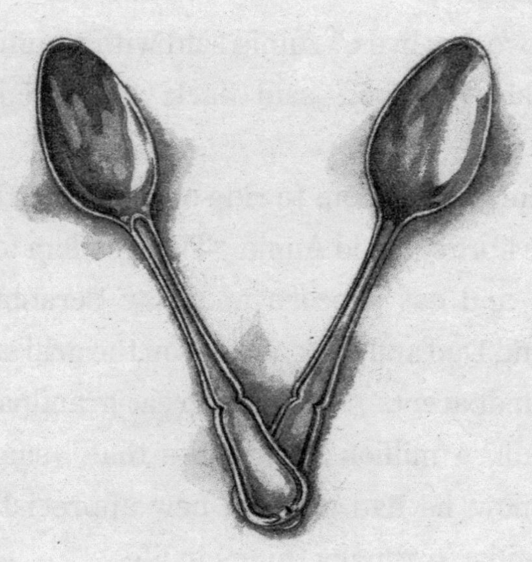

TRACK THE FACTS BEHIND JACK AND ANNIE'S MISSION

Turn the page to learn more about World War II.

More Information About World War II

World War II was fought all over the world from 1939 until 1945. The war involved more than thirty countries and was fought between two main groups of powers: the Allied powers and the Axis powers. The chief Allied powers were Great Britain, the Soviet Union, and the United States. The chief Axis powers were Germany, Italy, and Japan.

At the time of World War II, Germany was led by a brutal dictator named Adolf Hitler, who was the head of a political party called the Nazi Party.

Beginning in 1938, Hitler's Nazi forces quickly invaded many European countries, including Austria, Poland, the Netherlands, Belgium, Luxembourg, France, Denmark, Yugoslavia, Greece, and Norway.

In the summer of 1940, Germany's air force attacked Great Britain. But under the leadership of Prime Minister Winston Churchill, the British withstood the attack and defeated the Germans in the Battle of Britain. It was the first defeat for Germany in the war.

The United States did not become directly involved in World War II until 1941. On December 7, Japan bombed Pearl Harbor, a US naval base in Hawaii, and the next day, the United States declared war on Japan. Soon after, Hitler declared war on the United States. The United States joined the Allied powers and fought the Axis powers in many countries all over the world for the next four years.

World War II ended on September 2, 1945, when Japan was the last country to formally surrender to the Allies. The war lasted for six years and one day. It is estimated that during that time, 50 million to 85 million people lost their lives.

D-Day

On June 6, 1944, 150,000 Allied soldiers invaded the coast of Normandy in France to fight Hitler's army. D-Day was the largest land, air, and sea invasion in the history of the world. It became the turning point for World War II.

Spies and the Resistance

During World War II, spies were sent behind enemy lines to gather information for their side. In Great Britain, Prime Minister Winston Churchill formed a highly secret spy organization known as the SOE, which stood for **S**pecial **O**perations **E**xecutive. Both men and women were members of the SOE. They were ordinary people from all walks of life who were willing to risk their lives to defeat the Nazis.

In Nazi-occupied countries, there were also

many hidden groups known as the Resistance, who were trying to fight Hitler's army. Often working with Allied spies, Resistance groups used wireless radios to communicate secretly with Allied forces. They also resisted the invaders through acts of sabotage, such as blowing up rail lines used by the Nazi soldiers for traveling and for transporting weapons.

War Pigeons

During World War II, pigeons were used by both the Allied and Axis powers to carry messages across Europe. The pigeons were known as carrier pigeons or homing pigeons. They were used as couriers because they could fly at high altitudes and find their way home to their handlers many miles away. Soldiers and spies would place a message in a small canister attached to the pigeon's foot. Then the pigeon would carry the message home.

Great Britain had a National Pigeon Service, which used over 200,000 carrier pigeons. One of the most famous British pigeons was named

Commando. Commando flew more than ninety missions, carrying messages from agents in France to soldiers in Britain. He received a medal for his excellent service and today is remembered as one of the bravest creatures to ever serve in a war.

The German Enigma Machine

During any war, military messages are often intercepted by the enemy. In order to disguise their messages, military forces develop highly secret codes. They also train code breakers who try to decipher (or "crack") the enemy's codes.

Germany used one of the most complicated code systems of all time. The Germans created their code with a device called an Enigma machine. (*Enigma* means "puzzle.") The Enigma machine was a complicated typewriter designed to create a code that was nearly impossible to decipher. To make things even more difficult, the codes were changed every day.

Tanks

Tanks were invented by the British during World War I. Soon other countries also began using them. Thousands of tanks were built each month during the war. The early tanks could hardly move faster than a person walking. But by World War II, tanks had greatly improved—they were far more durable than the early tanks and could travel over very rough terrain.

Most countries used their tanks to carry powerful weaponry. But German tanks didn't have strong armor or firepower. This made them lighter and faster. The German tanks helped the Nazis develop a tactic known as blitzkrieg (which means "lightning war"). A blitzkrieg is an attack that uses speed and surprise to encircle and destroy an enemy. Germany was able to win many land battles using this technique.

Submarines and Aircraft Carriers

Much of World War II was fought on the ocean. The battleship had been the most powerful naval weapon in previous wars, but World War II marked the beginning of a new era—the invention of the submarine changed the way naval battles were fought. Both the Allies and the Axis powers used submarines. (German submarines were called U-boats.) The submarine was a valuable war machine, as it could travel underwater for short periods of time. Submarines used an underwater missile called a torpedo to sink large ships.

In addition to submarines, aircraft carriers were also new to naval warfare. These enormous ships carried airplanes that could take off from the ship, as well as land back on the ship. Most aircraft carriers could hold over thirty planes!

Airplanes

Airplanes played a larger role in World War II than in any previous war. Advanced technology made planes faster and more powerful. Unlike a tank or battleship, an airplane could travel anywhere. Taking off from airfields or from aircraft carriers, the plane could engage in combat over any sort of terrain or body of water.

Airplanes could also provide a bird's-eye view of enemy territory to help an army plan its attacks. And they could drop troops, spies, and

Jack and Annie parachuted from a plane called the Westland Lysander, shown here.

supplies behind enemy lines via parachute.

Fighter planes were especially important in World War II. Instead of dropping bombs like bomber planes, fighter planes faced each other in the air. There were almost 150 different kinds of fighter planes used during the war. One of the most famous of these planes was called the North American P-51 Mustang. It could fly higher and make sharper turns than any other plane.

The Holocaust

The Nazis were extremely prejudiced against the Jewish people. Under Hitler's leadership, the Nazis killed millions of Jewish people, as well as members of many other ethnic and political minority groups. To escape prison and death, some Jewish families went into hiding. They hid in caves or barns or under the floorboards of a friend's house. They had to be very secretive and quiet, often for days at a time.

The Diary of Anne Frank

In the Netherlands, a Jewish girl named Anne Frank and her family secretly moved into the building where her father worked. The price for helping someone wanted by the Nazis was death. In spite of this, coworkers of Anne's father helped the Frank family hide in the back of the building.

When they left their home, Anne and her family wore several layers of clothing because they did not want to be seen carrying suitcases into her father's work building. While they were hiding, they spent long hours every day being very quiet and hardly moving. Anne wrote in her diary to pass the time. She and her family lived there for two years, until they were captured.

After World War II ended, the whole world was horrified to learn of the full extent of the Nazi persecution of innocent people. People everywhere were deeply moved by the publication of Anne Frank's diary. Perhaps the most famous words from her diary are: "In spite of everything I still believe that people are really good at heart."

World War II greatly affected almost every country in the world, and so many terrible things happened that it is hard to fully comprehend its horrors. But over time, one young girl's diary has helped people to grieve for all those who senselessly died.

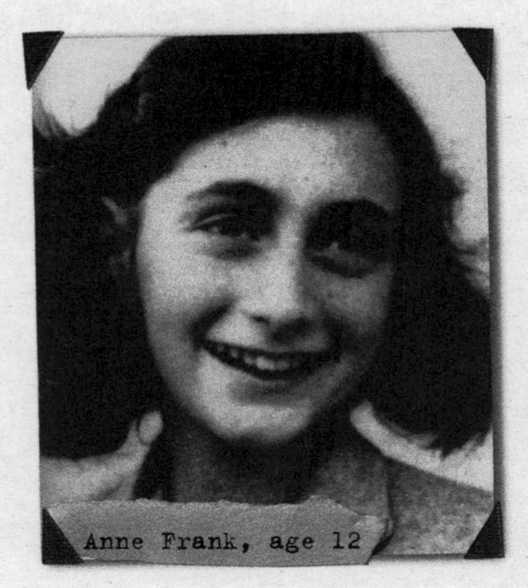
Anne Frank, age 12

Here's a special preview of

Magic Tree House®
MERLIN MISSION #27

NIGHT OF THE NINTH DRAGON

Available now!

CHAPTER ONE

That's It?

The day was cloudy and windy. Jack was sitting on the front porch, using a yellow marker to highlight a book called *Caring for Your New Puppy.*

"Fetch, Oki!" Annie shouted, throwing a ball across their yard.

Yip, yip! A scruffy black-and-white puppy raced after the ball and caught it in his mouth. "Bring it back!" Annie called. But Oki dashed away from her instead.

"He never does what you say," Jack said with a laugh.

"Yes, he does," said Annie. "He fetched! He just decided not to bring it back." She ran after Oki and wrestled the ball away from him. "Ready to go to the dog park now?" she called to Jack.

"Yep." Jack highlighted a paragraph about puppy dental care. Then he closed the book and dropped it into his pack along with his yellow marker. "All set."

"Did you pack supplies?" said Annie.

"Just his leash and water bowl," said Jack. "And some puppy treats." He pulled the leash out of his pack.

"Wait. Let's see if he'll walk with us on his own," said Annie.

"If I know him, he'll take off," said Jack.

"Come on, give him a chance. I've been working with him," said Annie. "Watch. Oki! Come!" The little dog ran to Jack and Annie.

"See?" said Annie as they started down the sidewalk.

"Do you really think he'll stay with us?" said Jack, putting the leash back in his pack.

“Sure,” said Annie.

“Hey, do you have any money?” Jack asked.

“What for?” said Annie.

“I thought we could stop at the pet store,” said Jack. “We need to get him a dog toothbrush and toothpaste. I was just reading that canine tooth care is very important. You have to—” Before Jack could finish, Oki yipped and dashed away down the sidewalk.

“Oki, wait! Oki!” shouted Annie. “Stay!”

But the puppy kept running. He crossed the street, bounded over the curb, and disappeared into the Frog Creek woods.

“I knew it!” Jack said.

“Oki!” Annie shouted. She and Jack raced into the woods after the puppy. Tree branches were waving in the wind. Dry autumn leaves shook and rustled.

“Oki!” yelled Jack.

“You were right!” wailed Annie. “We should have put him on the leash!”

“Don’t worry, we’ll find him,” said Jack.

"Oki!" they called. "Oki!"

Yip, yip!

"Did you hear that?" said Jack.

"Yes!" Annie and Jack took off running between the trees. They followed the yipping sounds—until they found the puppy at the base of a giant oak tree.

The magic tree house was nestled high in the treetop. The rope ladder was swaying from side to side.

"Good boy, Oki!" Annie said. She picked up the puppy and giggled as he licked her face. "How did you know it was back?"

"Teddy?" Jack called, looking up at the tree house. "Teddy?"

There was no answer, and no one looked down from the window.

"Let's climb up," said Annie. "There must be a message inside."

Yip? Yip?

"Yes, you're coming with us!" Annie said to Oki. "Here, get in Jack's bag." Jack took off his backpack, and Annie lowered the puppy inside. "Is that going to be too heavy?"

"No, he doesn't weigh much," said Jack, pulling on the pack. "Let's go, buddy." Jack carried Oki up the rope ladder, and Annie followed.

When they had all climbed into the tree house, Jack took off his pack and set it on the floor. Oki scampered out and began sniffing every corner.

"I don't see anything here," said Annie, looking around.

"Me neither," said Jack. There was no message from Merlin, no book from Morgan. "There's nothing here to tell us what to do."

Yip, yip, yip! Oki was looking out the window, barking at the woods.

Jack looked up and saw a scrap of paper floating on the wind. "Hey, is that our note?" he said.

"It must have blown out of the window!" said Annie. "I'll get it." She hurried back down the rope ladder. Oki kept barking as Annie chased after the paper and finally snatched it from the ground.

Annie read the note to herself and smiled.

Annie read the note to herself.

"What does it say?" Jack called.

"Good news!" said Annie.

"What? What is it?" said Jack.

"See for yourself!" said Annie. She scrambled back up the ladder and handed Jack the scrap of paper. "Our favorite place to visit."

Jack looked at the old-fashioned handwriting:

Dear Jack and Annie,

Please come to Camelot.

"That's it?" said Jack.

"It's good news, right?" said Annie.

"Yeah, but it doesn't look like Merlin or Morgan's handwriting, or Teddy's. . . . I don't understand. Who wrote this? And why?" said Jack.

"It doesn't matter," said Annie. "It's an invitation to Camelot! I love visiting Camelot, don't you?"

"Of course," said Jack. They had visited the kingdom many times. He loved its orchards and the Great Hall and Morgan's magnificent library. Most of all, he loved their friends in Camelot. "But something's weird."

"Don't worry, Jack. Let's just go," said Annie. "Get ready, Oki!" She pointed at the word *Camelot* on the note. "I wish we could go *there*!"

Yip! Yip!

Jack grabbed Oki and held him tightly.

The wind blew harder.

The tree house started to spin.

It spun faster and faster.

Then everything was still.

Absolutely still.

Magic Tree House®

#1: Dinosaurs Before Dark
#2: The Knight at Dawn
#3: Mummies in the Morning
#4: Pirates Past Noon
#5: Night of the Ninjas
#6: Afternoon on the Amazon
#7: Sunset of the Sabertooth
#8: Midnight on the Moon
#9: Dolphins at Daybreak
#10: Ghost Town at Sundown
#11: Lions at Lunchtime
#12: Polar Bears Past Bedtime
#13: Vacation Under the Volcano
#14: Day of the Dragon King
#15: Viking Ships at Sunrise
#16: Hour of the Olympics
#17: Tonight on the *Titanic*
#18: Buffalo Before Breakfast
#19: Tigers at Twilight
#20: Dingoes at Dinnertime
#21: Civil War on Sunday
#22: Revolutionary War on Wednesday
#23: Twister on Tuesday
#24: Earthquake in the Early Morning
#25: Stage Fright on a Summer Night
#26: Good Morning, Gorillas
#27: Thanksgiving on Thursday
#28: High Tide in Hawaii

Magic Tree House® Merlin Missions

#1: Christmas in Camelot
#2: Haunted Castle on Hallows Eve
#3: Summer of the Sea Serpent
#4: Winter of the Ice Wizard
#5: Carnival at Candlelight
#6: Season of the Sandstorms
#7: Night of the New Magicians
#8: Blizzard of the Blue Moon
#9: Dragon of the Red Dawn
#10: Monday with a Mad Genius
#11: Dark Day in the Deep Sea
#12: Eve of the Emperor Penguin
#13: Moonlight on the Magic Flute
#14: A Good Night for Ghosts
#15: Leprechaun in Late Winter
#16: A Ghost Tale for Christmas Time
#17: A Crazy Day with Cobras
#18: Dogs in the Dead of Night
#19: Abe Lincoln at Last!
#20: A Perfect Time for Pandas
#21: Stallion by Starlight
#22: Hurry Up, Houdini!
#23: High Time for Heroes
#24: Soccer on Sunday
#25: Shadow of the Shark
#26: Balto of the Blue Dawn
#27: Night of the Ninth Dragon

Magic Tree House® Super Edition

#1: World at War, 1944

Magic Tree House® Fact Trackers

Dinosaurs
Knights and Castles
Mummies and Pyramids
Pirates
Rain Forests
Space
Titanic
Twisters and Other Terrible Storms
Dolphins and Sharks
Ancient Greece and the Olympics
American Revolution
Sabertooths and the Ice Age
Pilgrims
Ancient Rome and Pompeii
Tsunamis and Other Natural Disasters
Polar Bears and the Arctic
Sea Monsters
Penguins and Antarctica
Leonardo da Vinci
Ghosts
Leprechauns and Irish Folklore
Rags and Riches: Kids in the Time of Charles Dickens
Snakes and Other Reptiles
Dog Heroes
Abraham Lincoln
Pandas and Other Endangered Species
Horse Heroes
Heroes for All Times
Soccer
Ninjas and Samurai
China: Land of the Emperor's Great Wall
Sharks and Other Predators
Vikings
Dogsledding and Extreme Sports
Dragons and Mythical Creatures
World War II

More Magic Tree House®

Games and Puzzles from the Tree House
Magic Tricks from the Tree House
My Magic Tree House Journal
Magic Tree House Survival Guide
Animal Games and Puzzles
Magic Tree House Incredible Fact Book